Angels
in
the
Rough

by Cece Whittaker

Easton One Productions
Absecon, New Jersey
www.CeceWhittakerStories.com
First Edition, 2020.

Cover Design by Jenifer Givner
Acapella Book Cover Design
acapellabookcoverdesign.com

-Dedication-

To my dear Friend & fellow Detective

Anna Mae Bensel,

with great love, gratitude, & admiration;

May our comic situations &

Abilities to laugh at ourselves never end!

Chapter One

The crystal angels on the shelves sparkled in the subdued light, their golden wing tips twinkling like the first stars of the night. Finding it impossible to accept the changes from the painfully recent past, Annie diRosa felt suspended in an enveloping confusion. So many things had changed between Christmas 1944 and only one month later, and as precious things seemed to fly out of her life she wished, longed for, cried for the days that had gone by.

"This is so hard," Annie said, brushing a stray tear from her face with the feather duster, then startling herself by poking a stray feather in her eye. She sighed impatiently and rubbed her eye. She hated crying, and she wasn't too fond of feather dusters either, just then. The shelves were fine, she decided, and the dust on the statues can wait. Christmas is over and I won't be getting too many customers now.

Still, she couldn't resist staring at the golden-lit angels on the shelves. They seemed to hold such promise. Their halos took her back to the shining night in December when the world was alight with happiness forever. Or so she thought.

It was Christmas night. She and Joan Foster, Bernice St. John, and Helen Ashenbach had all gathered for a warm Christmas dinner—lonely for their fellows who were far away fighting the war, fates undetermined. But then the magnificent events that brought them all together had filled the house with such joy, Annie was sure it would never end. Her dear, handsome, and brave Sylvester home again—how could it be? He had been injured, and ironically, so had she. They laughed at the irony, snuggling together under one of Helen's lovely afghans on her couch as the others there at Helen's house mingled, danced, and shared the golden holiday of Christmas.

Sylvester's eyes seemed never to leave her. They must have kissed a hundred times at least, she remembered. It was impossible to forget the warmth, the protection she felt with his arm around her. Even as she stood there in her lonely shop a month later, the thought of it made her catch her breath. How can love be so complete, she wondered, so all-consuming?

Annie had known then that they would never part, there were to be no more nights wondering where he was, if he were alive, or wounded, or worse. All would be perfect in the world. She was sure of it. And then?

She put away the feather duster, closed up the glass cabinets, felt the little catch click closed, and rested her hands on the counter. She tried to be strong. Annie hated crying. At least she hated it when it came out of her. Others could cry, but she would not. She would figure it all out, everything would be all right. Sylvester loved her. She knew that. She was sure of it. Just as she was sure they would never be apart again.

Oh why did he move up to that base? He had done his service, he was discharged, he could do what he wanted now—marry her! But instead, he went away.

An hour away! The tears came harshly then, and she covered her face as she cried, as if hiding. But only she knew her pain. She and God.

On the outskirts of Wrightstown, across from the Army base and inside a bright, single-level, rooming house whose halls smelt of tomatoes and basil, Lieutenant Bapini opened his wallet and took out the fifty dollars.

"Not too bad," he said smiling. "I think it has everything I need."

"We respect what you're doing," Mrs. Mifsud, the landlady said, eyeing his GI patch on the cast he still wore. "You fellas keep us safe. That's all we ask. And the rent you pay me will help me keep things up, Lieutenant."

"I appreciate it, "Ma'am," he said. "And you can call me Sylvester. Or Sly. Everybody does."

She smiled and closed the door, saying, "All right Sylvester. I'll let you get settled in."

Inside his new quarters, Sylvester felt the surge of energy that comes with a new adventure. But it was bittersweet. He had a nagging feeling that no matter how Annie had thrown off the news of his departure, she was hiding her real feelings. On the other hand, it could be nothing. She was tough to figure. Not that he was any picnic himself. Both of them seemed to have decided that guarded feelings were a sign of maturity and strength.

Maybe so, he thought nodding. Besides, if she'd wanted him to stick around, she would have said something. As it turned out, this move was essential, and there was nothing he could have done to get around it.

He slung his gunny sack onto the bed, opened it up, and dumped the contents into a pile. He could put those away later, he decided. He hung up his civilian suit bag in Mrs. Mifsud's tiny rooming house closet, barely fitting it in above the thin space allotted for his dress shoes.

He was grateful not to have to jam in several uniforms. But he missed the uniform. He missed the camaraderie. It had been only a month since he'd been home in the States. He remembered the excitement he and Bobby had felt on the ship, seeing Harry there and learning that they were going home, medically discharged. At the time, all they could think of was that they would be able to eat, they would not have to sleep in the rain or freezing temperatures. And that they would see their loved ones, the thought that had kept them going through those harrowing, painful, and uncertain months.

He sighed. That was the best part; getting to Helen's house on Christmas night, knowing that's where Annie would be. Harry had gone in first, alone. His wonderful wife, Helen, had just about passed out from the shock, but boy it was something to see. Sylvester remembered the couple of minutes he'd stood outside in the cold, just to create the effect that Harry was the only one coming in.

But he knew Annie was hoping he'd be there too, and it had been killing him to wait. When he'd charged through the door, as well as anyone with one bad leg could do, he'd embraced Annie with such force that they'd toppled over, laughing and crying for joy at the same time. He'd felt transported into a land of pure joy.

That is, until he'd noticed that she, too, was wearing a cast on her leg. It had fractured him to know not only had he been clumsy but that he might have hurt her. Mercifully, he'd done nothing and as they lay there laughing with the others staring down at them, he knew they'd created a memory that would last forever. It was one he would cherish as he trudged to the base and back through the cold this January and beyond. At least he wouldn't be alone, he thought smiling.

He opened up the curtains, noticing that his view from the one window he had was of a kind of meadow that he could envision cows or goats grazing in. It reminded him of the couple in Italy, where he'd taken a room earlier in the course of the War. He thought of them, wondering how they had survived, if they had survived. There were so many he had known, and so many he'd either served or been served by. He felt pangs of isolation then, yearning for the action, the sense of belonging, and the objectives shared with his buddies.

Sylvester shook it off, though, and stepping away from the window he busied himself at the little sink. The bathroom down the hall would be shared with the other boarders, but his room had a sink for washing up and a mirror with a cabinet built in behind it. I wonder if it's a two-way mirror, he thought chuckling to himself.

As he put away his things, discovering little built in cabinets and shelves along the way, his enthusiasm returned. It would be exciting, he knew, to work this new job. "Job," he said out loud smiling. Not so much of a job as an occupation. His entire focus from college had been shifted due to his time in the military. He would never have known the excitement of learning enemy secrets simply by asking the enemy directly, as they had done in Italy.

But even more he felt the thrill of this new challenge, the one he had left the comfort of gentle Abbottsville for, and in which he could only hope to succeed, since he had no experience and no training. Yet that fact only served to make the endeavor more exciting.

He hadn't thought to bring a bedroll, but luckily Mrs. Mifsud had provided a deep downy comforter and pillow on the little bed that was to be his. Both were immaculate, as was the entire room.

Unpacking a small bag with washcloth, soap, razor, and comb, Sylvester took a look around himself and nodded. Everything would be all right. He would make the situation turn out. It had to, he thought wistfully, but only for a moment. Then, grabbing his Army issue field jacket, he set out on foot for the train station to meet his buddy.

Back at the New Jersey shore, Joan Foster stepped off the bus from work and shivered in the icy cold January wind of Abbottsville.

"Shew!" she said to herself, pulling her scarf around her face. "Who would ever think being inside that old rattletrap could be better than something. But I sure wouldn't mind if it traveled down these side streets!"

Joan's job as a secretary had been reinstated at the beginning of that month. It had been happy news because her savings had just about run out, and as things stood, she still needed to earn herself a living. The previous summer she had lost the job, but with the promise that if things picked up again, she would be called back. The happy news had come just after the holidays. And suddenly, everything was right in the world for Joan.

She scurried down the street toward home, thinking of what she would throw together for dinner for Annie and herself. She and Annie shared a little house a couple of blocks from the main street in Abbottsville. In the short time they had spent together, they had grown very close. Joan and Annie shared the dream of a happy home with a loving man, children, and a solid future. And now they were so close, Joan thought with excitement.

Why, when Dick gets back from visiting his mother, I bet we'll set a date and before you know it, I'll be Mrs. Richard Thimble. Joan felt as if her life had finally begun to blossom.

As she opened the door to their little house on Arden Road, she quickly scurried over to turn on the heat. The furnace wumped and vibrated and eventually caught its breath and kept a steady whir as Joan took off her coat and scarf and replaced them with a heavy sweater.

She hurried to the kitchen, put on an apron, got out a casserole dish and began pulling things out of the vegetable drawer.

"Let's see," she said, tossing things into her apron, "carrots, celery. We've got six potatoes. Hmm, how about two and we'll chop those up into smaller pieces, some parsley, and one parsnip." She closed the drawer with a bang and carried those she had collected in her sagging apron to the counter. She peeled the carrots, potatoes, and the parsnip, cleaned the celery, and chopping everything up into bite-sized pieces, mixed them together in the casserole dish. Sprinkling bits of parsley, and then carefully slicing a small wedge from the pound of butter in the icebox, she added it along with some water, salt & pepper, covered the dish and put it in the oven. It wouldn't be a hearty meal like the ones they'd scrimped their savings for over the holidays, but it would be good, she thought.

She leaned back against the counter, happy to be home and safe inside, shielded from the wind. She closed her eyes remembering that first moment she had caught sight of Dick after all that time away, as he and Bob and Laureen had come through the door at Helen's house on Christmas night. Even a month later, her heart still rose like a helium balloon at the thought of him. He was so handsome. But it wasn't his looks that had her spellbound. It was just him, his deep magnetism. She felt sorry for the women who didn't have him. How could they stand it, she thought. And the dramatic reunion had been heightened by the fact that until that very moment, Joan had been struggling with the very real possibility that Dick had died from wounds suffered in France. The War had taken a deep toll on its southern Jersey citizens. Joan's tears were not shed alone. And while she was comforted by the love and support of her dear friends Annie, Helen, and Bernice, she had walked around in a dark despair she hoped never to see again.

But then, suddenly, with the light and promise of Christmas, there he was! Long recovering not in Abbottsville or Atlantic City's hospital, but in Oklahoma. And he was on his feet, thin—very thin— but recovering from a type of septicemia that might

very well have taken his life. Joan's prayers of
thanksgiving for that miracle overwhelmed even her
earlier prayers for his safe return.

He had swallowed her up in his warm, still
muscular arms, holding her close, his Army uniform
loose-fitting but pressed and smelling of his
captivating aftershave lotion. That night they had
danced, sat close eating their magnificent Christmas
feast, watched the others dance, celebrated the happy
return of so many, listened to stories and laughed and
cried until the night had almost dissolved into morning
light.

No one wanted to leave. No one wanted the day to
ever come to an end. But when Bob and Laureen were
ready to go and Dick had to leave, they'd embraced in
a way that was like speaking promises. She had seen in
Dick's eyes a happiness that matched the way she felt
herself. Such love she had never known was possible.
There was suddenly shape and life to the meaning of
the word forever.

She heated the tea kettle and just as it started to
purr, the front door opened.

"Good timing, Annie," she called. "I've just got the
water hot for tea."

"It's not Annie," Bernice called out. "It's the big bad
wolf."

"Well, if it is," Joan answered, "you won't find any
tasty grandmothers in here."

"I'm just coming to eat your dinner," Bernice said
as she entered the kitchen. "Oh, tea! Thank you, Lord!"
She plopped down into a chair at the kitchen table.
"But I'll share with any grandmothers in need."

Joan laughed and put a cup and saucer out for Bernice and Annie and herself. "It's just about ready," she said. "Dark out there, isn't it?"

"Yeah," said Bernice. "I see you've got the curtains pulled."

"On the days that we work, we don't even open them," Joan said. "What's the point? By the time we get home it's almost dark anyway."

"Hopefully before long this awful War will be over with and you can leave the curtains open all 24 hours," Bernice said, twirling the cup slowly in its saucer.

It was 1945 and the War had dragged on by then for over three years, washing away so many hopes of happiness and peace. The women knew their own sorrows, which were painful enough. But the news that had begun to filter in from across the ocean shocked and terrified them. A large part of Annie's family resided in Italy, but each girl felt the loyalty to their European neighbors.

Aside from the Nazi atrocities, they had learned that most Europeans did not have very much to eat, and many were cold, with no fuel for heat. Grateful for the safe return of their own loved ones, they still ached for the many that still suffered horribly. They continued their support, perhaps even more fervently, for the Allied soldiers who served, and prayed daily for them to win the War and for the suffering to come to an end.

"Sometimes I wish," Bernice said, staring at her empty teacup, "that I could personally hand a nice hot drink and giant sandwich to someone in need. Or bring a pitcher of milk and a batch of cookies to some of those poor orphaned children."

Joan nodded, pouring the tea over the leaves into the pot. "I know, Bernice," she said soberly. "I guess with the happiness we've found in the last little while, the suffering around us feels all that much more intense."

"Yeah, because of the extreme," Bernice said, her soft brown eyes glistening. "When we were worried and praying for the men to be safe and come home, we were in the same boat, or so we thought. But now. . . " She drifted off for a moment. "Ah well, let's say grace for the tea anyway."

Just then, the door opened again and Annie called, "It's me, Joanie."

"And Bernice," called Bernice.

"And Bernice," mimicked Annie.

"Don't make fun of me," Bernice warned, "I might put something in your tea."

"You got tea in there?" Annie asked, putting away her coat.

"It's yours," said Joan. "I just filled the pot, come on in."

"I'm coming, I'm coming," Annie said. "I've got a bone."

Joan looked at Bernice, giggling. "Did she say she has a bone?"

"Yes, I did," said Annie in the doorway. "It's a neck bone, comes in a bunch of pieces like a puzzle."

"Oh that will make excellent soup," Joan said.

"I know it! Why do you think I snatched it up? Oh, thank you, Lord. The tea looks great."

"That's what Bernice said," Joan said giggling.

They sat down together, said a quick prayer of thanks, and began to sip their tea, Bernice's with sugar,

Annie's with milk, and Joan's just as it came out of the pot.

"I put in a vegetable casserole, sort of," said Joan.

"Oh, that's good. The soup won't be ready til late tonight, and we can have it tomorrow. But I think I'll start it soon so I'm not up all night with it."

"How were things at the shop?" Joan asked. "Any customers?"

"Just one. She wanted a pack of holy cards for her students." Annie's shop, filled with statues, rosaries, pictures, and sacred keepsakes did not rattle the economics of Abbottsville's Chamber of Commerce. But it was a living for a single person, especially around important holy days.

"Slow these days, huh?" Bernice asked.

"Yeah, and I don't mind. It's good so I can put things away and sort of get caught up."

"You doing okay?" Joan said cautiously.

"Oh yeah, you mean Sylvester going away? Yeah. I understand. Let's get the soup started so by the time dinner's ready, it'll be on to cook." Annie stood up and put on an apron.

Joan and Bernice exchanged glances.

"I'll go and get the mail," Joan said. "The salt & pepper are already out."

Annie busied herself at the stove, quickly assembling the basic bit of oil, chopped garlic and a dried basil. She started adding the bone, section by section, stirring and adding water as she did so.

"Mmm, smells good," said Bernice.

"Yeah, that's the garlic," Annie said. "I love a neck bone soup. They say it has healing qualities if you're sick." She peeled two of the remaining potatoes and chopped them into pieces.

They stood watching it bubble for a while, and then Annie added another bone.

"You know you oughta put this in," Bernice said, picking up a bone from the middle of the column.

"What's that?" demanded Annie, not fond of uninvited contributions to her soup pot.

"It's a funny bone," Bernice answered, plunking it into the pot.

"A what?"

"A funny bone," said Bernice, taking over the stirring. "I read that if you cook these in, you get laughing stock."

Annie paused for a moment, and then began to giggle in spite of herself. Through her laughter, she shoved Bernice on the shoulder, saying, "You're such an idiot."

Bernice continued to stir, straight-faced. "I only know what I read," she said.

Joan returned with the mail. "Which would you like, the heating bill or the JC Penney catalog?"

"Oh put that in the bathroom," Annie said. "The catalog, I mean. You can have the heating bill."

"Thanks a lot!" Joan stopped short. "Oh gosh, look at this," she said holding up the catalog. "Valentine's Day!"

Chapter Two

Next day, while Annie put away the soup, Helen and Harry Ashenbach, living just around the corner, were finishing up breakfast.

"All right, I'll see you this evening, then," said 57-year-old Helen Ashenbach as she kissed her husband Harry goodbye. "Be sure and take your coat. It's very cold out." She ran her hands through his hair, just to feel its softness, but pretended she was smoothing it for him.

He caught her hand in his and gave her a daring look. "Okay, Mrs. Ashenbach, don't start that up, or you'll be making up that bed a second time this morning!"

Helen laughed and shoved him away. "You better get going, Captain, oh excuse me, Major. Your public awaits."

Harry took a last sip of coffee. "You make the best darn coffee, woman," he said scrunching up his face. "Makes me not wanna leave."

"Oh, it's the coffee, is it?"

Harry moved closer to her. "Well, if you want to find out. . ."

Helen giggled, gave him another kiss, and went to the hall closet to get his coat. "Better not tempt me," she said.

After he had left, Helen leaned against the door, closing her eyes peacefully. She was a lucky woman. How she loved Harry! And now he was home — hopefully this time to stay. She had thought he was there permanently that same time last year, when suddenly he'd been called down to "train." Well, training had lasted about 6 weeks, and he wasn't doing the training, he was getting the training. She shook her head, remembering the disappointment when she had learned that he had been returned to the European theatre.

Harry Ashenbach had been elevated to officer status following what the girls and she referred to as "secret stuff." In actual fact, Harry had been a courier, later graduated to a spy of sorts. But now that was behind him, as he had formally stepped out of the uniform. She nodded, convincing herself. He can't still be in the Army — he doesn't even wear the uniform anymore.

Of course there are folks not wearing the uniform that do other things, she thought. "Oh forget it!" she said out loud. "Whatever will be, will be."

Just then came a series of assorted knocks on the door. She smiled. That could only be the girls.

She opened the door to Joan, Annie, and Bernice, standing there in comical poses. "What are you knocking for?" Helen asked. "You live here, or you did for a month!"

As they crowded into the living room, Annie shook her head sadly. "I hate to move all our things back," she said. "It feels so permanent."

"I never said you had to," said Helen. "Harry and I have the three daughters we never had when you gals are here. Take off your coats. I'm making coffee."

"Ooooh, coffee!" said Joan. "That sounds marvelous."

"Yes, it does!" Annie agreed.

"You got cream, too?" Bernice asked.

"Hey gals, I got it all," Helen said laughing. "Grab a chair. We can catch up on what's going on."

"I don't know about the rest of us, but it's pretty clear you and Harry are doing a lot of catching up," Annie said. "Look at that smile on your face!"

"Annie!" Helen said.

"Yeah, Annie, what did you mean by that?" Bernice asked, smiling.

"Nothing bad, I just meant you must be swapping lonely hearts stories," Annie said. "Why? What did you think I meant?"

Joan giggled and shook her head.

"Well," Helen answered, "you're right about that. We have had so much fun. It's been like a dream. I almost feel guilty having such happiness, but then I remember what's led up to it, and I don't feel that guilty."

"No, you deserve this time," Joan said solemnly. "Don't ever doubt that."

Helen smiled and covered Joan's hand with hers.

"She's right," said Annie.

"Absolutely," said Bernice.

"We've still got to earn our stripes," said Annie.

"Stripes! Ew!" said Joan. "Plaids, but not stripes."

Bernice burst out laughing.

"What's so funny?" Joan demanded.

"She meant like non-com's stripes, you know, military promotions," Bernice said. "After all, he got raised to Major on his way out."

"Oh, oh, okay," said Joan.

"Dick's out of the Army what, four weeks, and you've already forgotten?" Annie teased.

"No, I think it's just that I just had my head in the fabric box before we came over. I was hoping to put something together for Valentine's in case there's a dance."

"There is a dance," said Helen. "I've been slacking off since Harry got home, but I'm supposed to be putting together the hall and decorations. Any little elves in the room want to join me?"

"I will," said Annie, "provided I can work around the shop schedule."

"Yes, it's only a couple of days a week," Helen said. "I don't know about you, though, Joan. Since you've started back to work full time."

"Well, I can do what you need me to do in the evenings," Joan said. "I don't wanna be the only slacker!"

Bernice laughed. "Joanie, the day anybody calls you a slacker is the day the world throws up."

Joan burst out laughing. "Throws up?"

Annie shook her head. "Bernice, that is just so gross."

"I made her laugh, didn't I?"

"I'll be sure to include you, Joan, in whatever you like," Helen said. "And we won't need any global ailments to assist us."

"Before we get into that—" Annie started.

"Oh, yes, you want to gather your things—" Helen said.

"No, I meant something else, but maybe we should."

"I don't think it's necessary," said Helen. "Truth be told, that spare room has never been happier than when you three were here last month."

"It was so much fun!" Joan said. "Like a never-ending slumber party. And Christmas—after being together and then having the happy shock of our lives all together, what a fantastic and unforgettable way to celebrate Christmas."

"It was," Helen said.

For a moment, all four women were lost in thoughts.

"Well, as far as I'm concerned," Helen said, "if there are things you don't need at home or are duplicates of things you already have, I'd just as soon you left them here. We can have slumber parties whenever we want, at the spur of the moment. I will buy a few extra toothbrushes and leave some towels in the bedroom and it will always be open to you girls—in any combination," she added smiling.

"Well I'm all for it!" Annie said.

"Me, too," said Joan.

"I might just move in permanently," Bernice teased.

"It would be fine with me!" Helen said.

"Yeah, but not with Harry!" Annie laughed.

"You know, I think he's loved it, too," Helen said thoughtfully. "He asked why everyone moved out so quickly and I told them they thought he'd want it that way, and he said no. It was like a family and he loved it."

"It really is like a family," Joan said. "It's been wonderful to have everyone here and our extended family, the men and friends. Since Mom and Dad decided to spend a whole year in Indiana, I've really felt like this was home."

"I've got family right over in Atlantic City," Annie said, "but I feel the same way."

"Me, too," said Bernice. "I think it has to do with how much we've shared over the past year—hard to believe it's been only about a year and a half since the St. Nick's dance, hasn't it?"

"And a year and a few months since the men shipped out," Annie said. "What a horrible, horrible day that was."

Again, they found themselves lost in thought. It was true. Annie could still see Sylvester's deep brown eyes, brows slanting down in pain and sorrow as he said goodbye to her at their diner. He'd worn his leather jacket that night, and he smelled of leather and after shave. He'd been determined to serve, determined to do his part, even though he was so close to graduating college. But he would be out of harm's way, as they described it, doing engineering work to suit his major study. He would be one of the advance men, laying out plans for landing strips, buildings, and roadways before the troops arrived.

And then, to everyone's surprise, he was suddenly in a completely different specialty. One of the men in his platoon had mentioned to another that Sylvester spoke Italian. The information was passed around to the Special Communications Division, and before he knew it, Lt. Sylvester Bapini was no longer an Army Engineer, but a Linguistics Specialist.

It was there that Sly had met his buddy Bobby. The two of them then trained in interrogation together and traveled to Italy to perform field investigations and interview prisoners of war. It was there, in Italy, where they both got to know Harry Ashenbach, one of the Army's new operatives under guise of a heavy equipment repairman.

Annie had heard some of the stories about the men's adventures in Italy, but there were many she had no interest in hearing, which was fortunate. Neither Sly nor Harry had any interest in telling them. She concentrated on the more recent past, seeing her handsome fiancé tear toward her on Christmas night with such urgency that he knocked her over. She laughed out loud for a second, startling Joan and Bernice.

"Oh Joan, Bernice," she said. "Sorry about that! I was just remembering getting tackled on Christmas."

"That was so funny!" Joan said laughing.

Bernice smiled. The rest of them had stood there laughing, watching first with fear then realizing Annie was all right, great amusement at Sylvester's concern, and someone had made a comment about laying on the ground together or something. She had been sitting next to her dear friend Henry, another soldier who was still recovering, but had been well enough to make it to Midnight Mass and then, that night to Christmas Dinner at Helen's.

Her relationship with Henry had been more of a light romance in high school, but over the last year and a half, Bernice had felt called to enter the sisterhood. Much to her disappointment, she had been told that she would first need to spend a year discerning, making sure that that life was what she truly wanted. And while many things had come along to cause a delay in her plans, her heart was still very much committed to serving God as a nun. It was after she had inherited a great sum of money from her uncle that she realized she also wanted to become a nurse. And at that point in time, her plan to study was just starting to unfold.

"Well Father Bertrand and Monsignor Kuchesky didn't say anything," Bernice said, remembering the sight of Annie and Sly on the floor together. "I guess they were willing to give you two the benefit of the doubt."

"Well, I should say so, considering she was the victim!" Helen laughed. "How is your leg, by the way, Annie? I notice you're not using the cane or anything anymore."

"No, I never really needed that. They just wanted me to have something. It healed really fast."

"You think you could get away from Sylvester if you had to?" Bernice teased.

"The question is, could he outrun me?" Annie said. "He's still struggling. Poor guy. Twice wounded in the same leg."

"He's really lucky that he's made of such strong stuff," Joan said. "Not everybody would heal like that. He is blessed."

"We all are blessed," said Helen.

"Yes, we are!" all three girls answered in unison, then burst out laughing.

"Let's go straighten up the bedroom and see what we can do with all of your things," Helen said.

It was an easy arrangement and in less than half-hour, whatever needed taking was packed, and most of the things they might need were put in the second bathroom. Helen even laid out a set of towels on each bed and the cot.

"I love this little angel statue," Joan said.

"That one has a match in my room," Helen said. "Let me show you."

When stood together, the pair of angels seemed to be guarding the gates of Heaven. One in a long golden coat of armor, which Joan supposed to be St. Michael, and the other in white. Maybe that's the Angel Gabriel, she thought. The faces were finely chiseled, with proportional features and high cheekbone and strong jaws. They had long, arching wings lined in gold and robes that seemed to fall gently in folds around them.

"They should be somewhere special," Joan said. "They are too beautiful not to show."

"We'll put them up here," Helen said, lifting them up and placing them on a glass shelf above the dresser. "They can shine in plain sight right there."

Later, after Helen had poured everyone a second cup of coffee, they sat in the living room planning what would come next.

"It's funny," Joan said, "the men are home, and yet we're still making plans for volunteer work. Not that I don't want to—but I thought our next planning pow wows would be for someone's wedding." She winked at Annie, sure that Annie would smile, and she did, but

Joan was sure she detected a wince before the smile. "Of course there's no rush," she said quickly.

"We've got loads to do!" Helen said with ambiguous enthusiasm.

Annie was grateful. That Helen doesn't miss a trick, she thought. "That's for sure!" she said.

Joan was a little puzzled, but happy that her friends were filled with enthusiasm. "I love working together with you guys," she said.

"Me, too," said Bernice. "This is the best part of our friendship. Doing all this good stuff."

"Gosh Bernice," said Annie, "You're so doggone eloquent."

Joan and Helen laughed.

"Thank you, Annie," said Bernice.

As Helen thumbed through the binder that held her collection of outlines and suggestions from previous events, Joan leaned back in her chair with an expression of curiosity. "So Helen," she said, "what's it like having your man back in the house after all this time? Is it so great you can't believe it? Do you worry that it isn't real?"

The other girls moved closer, eager for her answer.

Helen looked up from her book, surprised at the question. "Well, the answer might surprise you," she said. "You girls know how much I love Harry. You know how hard it was for me, for all of us, worrying, knowing nothing, having to set aside our regular lives all those months, years. But living alone for that amount of time, you have to fend for yourself, take out the trash, pay the bills, fix the can opener, things like that. It makes you become more self-reliant. And with that comes a certain amount of independence.

"It's good you asked that question because you'll need to know this to keep things happy in your marriages, and also in your life, Bernice, as it changes, as well. In relationships, especially in marriage, you have to depend on each other. If you don't, you're just two people sharing a house. So when one becomes independent of the other, that person starts to overreach the relationship sort of boundaries.

"Well, of course when Harry went away, that had to be the case for me. And girls, it was also the case for Harry. He didn't have anyone doing his wash or helping put his meals together, aside from the other stuff."

The girls giggled.

"So both of us have to kind of readjust to being part of a twosome again. It's not that hard this time, but the first time he left for the War, that was very, very difficult. You'll hear about ladies who went to work while their husbands were away, and how hard it is for the two of them after that because money plays a role in independence, too.

"But happily, although we have to adjust a little bit, and get used to talking a whole lot more!" she laughed. "We are just so happy to be back together, and I think while he still wants to be doing something, Harry's desire to travel is pretty well quenched."

"I hope so, Helen," Annie said a little too sincerely.

Helen's and her eyes met, and Annie knew she had a friend who understood. She took a deep breath and let it out.

"He's got to be tired of it by now!" Joan said. "He's been just about everywhere in the world!"

"Yeah, now Helen's going to want to go to Europe!" Bernice said.

"Not any time soon!" Helen said.

"Okay," Annie said, feeling more enthusiastic. "Let's see what's what with this St. Valentine's Day dance!"

Chapter Three

Bernice St. John sat at her kitchen table, pen in hand, with a collection of intimidating forms in front of her. One of them was entitled St. Vincent's School of Nursing in thick dark letters, followed by rows of questions that looked to Bernice like the principal demanding to know where she was during science class.

She'd read the background to St. Vincent's, how they wanted very strong science and math students. She read that part twice. Math? Is that to keep a good count of the patients? It was all very confusing. She was happy to go through with it though, if it meant she could then learn what she wanted to learn and get her nursing certification.

She picked up another form. The Capital Nursing Institute. It was another school that seemed to indicate that in order to learn, you had to already have learned.

"How do you manage this?" Bernice said out loud. "Maybe there's pre-nursing school somewhere."

But throughout the morning, she couldn't identify one school that seemed to welcome an eager student who wasn't already educated in nursing.

At lunchtime, her mother came home. "How's the application process going?" she asked. "Almost finished?"

Bernice sighed. "I can't seem to find a place that I can even apply to. They all seem to want A-students in math and science. I didn't do so well in high school, but I want to learn now."

Mrs. St. John nodded. "That's why I never did go to school and worked in the cafeteria instead." She took out the peanut butter and jelly and began to make herself a quick sandwich.

"It seems like they should have some kind of training so that you can qualify for school," Bernice said. "There must be lots of girls like me. Maybe the arts school idea we had last year should be a science school."

"You mean with experiments and Bunson burners? Are we out of waxed bags?" asked Mrs. St. John.

"Yeah. I don't know what they teach in science schools. I never went to one." Bernice closed the last application, put down her pen and sighed.

Mrs. St. John took a bite of her sandwich, and with her coat still on, grabbed her handbag and headed out the door. "That's true," she said over her shoulder. "Get some more bags, would you?"

Bernice looked up in time to see the door slam closed. "Okay," she said to the empty kitchen. "I guess I should be used to this by now."

She leaned back on the chair and stared at the ceiling pondering her plan to become a nurse. Was it all just another wild idea? Taking care of her injured friend, Henry, had been so uplifting, but would it always be that way? And how could you tell? There were so many questions about feelings, convictions, and the difference between them. How do I know, she thought, if this a real desire or a passing fancy? You can love what you're doing one minute, and then it's just drudgery the next. How would I feel taking care of a crotchety old man who yelled at me all the time? I've sure seen plenty of them in the hospitals. Or what about the ones that get sick all over the place?

Oh, I don't know, she thought. What about the way it feels though when you can make someone feel better, get someone comfortable, give someone a clean face and hands to make them feel fresh? How about caring for newborn babies? There are so many questions.

She stood up to stretch her legs and headed to the back window facing Henry's street. Caring for him had meant making a friend's life comfortable, and eventually, better. It had been something so special. Now that he was mended and strong again, and pursuing his own calling at the monastery, she wasn't needed anymore. She missed him, and she missed the warm, laughing friendship they had shared. It was caring for him that had made her take an interest in nursing to begin with.

With him gone, though, and that part of her life ended, how much did she really want to be an actual nurse? What part of that profession would involve caring for someone who would get better like Henry did? Or would she only be caring for people who were dying?

"Maybe this isn't the day for this," she said out loud, observing the rain coming across the patio. "That sideways rain is always depressing."

As she made herself a sandwich, grateful for the food that in her house was now so plentiful, she remembered that she had agreed to meet with the temporary fellow working the grocery store—her grocery store. With her surprise inheritance the previous summer, that little grocery was the one thing that made good sense to her and to the town just then. But she had not been a good manager of it.

She smiled remembering how little she'd known about getting supplies for her store and how she'd been lucky enough to keep the previous owner on to run it. He'd shown her the ropes, and while she'd learned plenty, she still felt unsure of how to proceed when he was gone. There were so many details!

She felt she had a friend in Bob McGarrett, though, who had taken her by the hand and shown her that records needed to be kept in an orderly and regular fashion. You couldn't save them all up in a collection of places and then somehow come up with the figures you needed at month's end. Both she and the previous owner stood to learn a little in that area, she thought.

Bob and Laureen, dear friends whom she'd met through Joan, were engaged and getting married, was it May? Sometime soon, she knew that. She wondered how they would do together. It had been a rough road for them the preceding fall. While she was caring for Henry and helping him become restored to strength,

Laureen had been miserable. Bob would not see her, even though he was right there in the nearby hospital.

But their love had won out, she thought fondly. No small thanks for Father Bertrand, one of Bernice's favorite people in the world. Father was a veteran of an earlier war or two, and he knew how things affected men. But it was his compassion and clear vision that really moved Bob to understand what he was suffering from. He had never wanted to shut himself away, but he had not been able to pull himself out of it. With Father's understanding and serious soul searching, and of course Laureen's love and understanding, they had weathered that awful period. And now, thought Bernice, the reward for all of that pain and suffering, all that tenacity, even hard work. That's how it should be.

But now what? They were getting married and Bob was out of the service. They had discussed Bob's coming to work on Bernice's books, but that wasn't enough to keep a home. It was then that the idea hit her. Bob could manage the store! Ah, at least I have one good answer for my problems today! And Bernice headed out the door to find Joan and tell her about her idea.

Dick Thimble was still recovering his strength when he arrived at home in Washington, D.C. His mother had been so pleased to see him, but the loss of his father during his time away had taken a toll on her. It was good that he had left her his pension and a savings account, but she had slowed down herself, and spent most of her days visiting another old widow friend. Dick knew he was loved, but he felt somewhat displaced. He also felt a need to be on his own. If that weren't enough, he missed Joan desperately.

Their few weeks together had been glorious. It was the most time they'd been able to see each other since first meeting over a year before. He had bunked with Bob at Laureen's parents' house right in town. Bob and Laureen, Dick and Joan, almost every day, walking in the cold all bundled up, stopping for a hot chocolate, visiting their friends. Then Joan had gotten her job back full time, and they had seen each other instead for dinners at Joan & Annie's, or with everyone at Helen and Harry Ashenbach's. So many wonderful times, he thought, smiling.

How he had become so fortunate to find such a wonderful woman, and her wonderful friends, he could not fathom. He had never dreamed he could be so happy. And he longed for the day he could see Joan again.

But as he sat there at his mother's kitchen table, he wondered how that would ever happen. He certainly couldn't stay with his buddy's girlfriend's parents again, as great as that had been. But he needed a job, and until the money came from his government issue service, he wasn't sure what he would do for funds. His father had left him several bonds, and while Dick hated to cash them, he felt he should do so at least to get him started. But they were not enough to live on for very long.

As he puzzled over things, it occurred to him that his buddy might know where he could find work, and more specifically, somewhere near Joan. He began to write.

Hey Buddy, he began, such a great time I could never have imagined like the time I spent with you, your doll and her family — not to mention my own sweet Joan. I've been here just a week, and it occurs to me that I should make arrangement to return to that vicinity. While I would be happy to immediately grab a train, I'm concerned about my prospects for housing, job, and food—some of the more basic issues. Any thoughts—and no more sponging off of your wonderful soon to be in-laws. I've got to stand on my own two feet, at least the best I can at the moment.

The men shared wound humor. Dick's initial injury had been to the left posterior cheek, a great source of humor to his buddies, until the wound had turned septic. Bob's wound was initially more serious and almost involved the amputation of his leg. But luckily, he kept the leg and continued to recover rapidly.

But it was more the camaraderie the two shared that bound them together. Friends before joining the service, they had grown even more dependent on each other in battle, and ultimately formed a brotherhood that would bind them for life.

Dick walked to the post office to mail the letter on 16th Street.

Right around that time, Bernice tapped on Laureen's door.

"Hi!" said Laureen, "come on in."

"Thanks," said Bernice. "I hope this isn't too short notice."

"Not at all. In fact, Bob is helping dad in the garage and they'll be stopping for something to drink soon, I'm sure. Have a seat. I've got the fire going."

"Oh that's nice and cheerful!" Bernice said. "I won't stay long, but let me get in here close. There's nothing like a fire on a cold day."

"Or a cold night," said Laureen.

"Yes! I planned to come over with Joan but I'd forgotten she's at work. I'm glad for her, but I got used to her being around all the time."

"Me too," said Laureen. "I miss her a lot but we've still got the weekends, and who knows how long she'll be working anyway." Her eyes danced.

"Yeah!" Bernice agreed. "I bet not too long!"

Just then Bob tapped on the doorway. "Is this private?" he asked.

"No, come in, Bob," Bernice said. "You are actually the reason I wanted to come over."

Laureen stood up and shielded him dramatically. "No—sorry, he's taken," she said giggling.

"Oh shucks. Too late!" Bernice said.

Bob sat down, putting his arm around Laureen. "Is everything okay? I mean with Joan and Annie and all?"

"Yes, yes, everybody's fine," she assured him. "It's actually me. I need help."

"Oh?"

"Remember when I asked for your advice in straightening out that mess of an accounting system?"

"Oh yeah!" Bob laughed.

"Well, as you probably remember, the original owner is still managing for me, until I get a replacement."

"And he's messed up the books again!"

"Well, I don't know, possibly," Bernice said. "I never thought of that. But what I have to do, you see, since he has definitely decided to retire, is get a manager to take over. A better one than me, for sure, and even better than him. Someone who can learn quickly, is organized, is available, and wants a job in a situation that could grow."

Laureen's eyes glowed.

Bob smiled broadly.

"Anyone in mind?" Laureen asked, looking at Bob.

Bernice smiled, "Yes. I thought of you, Bob. You're so organized, and you and Dick both have retail experience. I thought maybe you could take it over and get yourself situated, you know, before the wedding and all."

Bob put forth his hand, and grabbed Bernice's, then said, "What the hell!" and gave her a big hug. "Of course I'm interested! A job, honey, you hear that? We can set a date!"

Laureen and he stood, embracing in earnest, each thinking of their lives together and how all of that would now be possible.

Bernice began to feel a little outside of things, and even though she was not as well acquainted with Laureen as she was with Annie, Joan, and Helen, the clown in her couldn't help embracing the two of them and saying, "We'll never part!"

Bob guffawed, and Laureen, startled at first, then laughing said, "Yes, the three of us, forever!" She looked at Bob, "This calls for a celebration!"

Bob put up his hand. "No," he said, "remember what we said. Every penny we have has to be saved, saved, saved."

"How about a nice dinner all of us together?" said Bernice.

"I don't think Sylvester is home, and we know Dick has gone back to DC," Laureen said, "but we could have one with a smaller gang!"

"Let's pass the word around anyway," Bernice said, "and thank you, Bob. This takes a giant load off my mind! We'll start making the transition later in the week, if that's okay with you."

"The sooner the better!"

That night, as Joan rode home on the bus, she thought about Annie. She says she understands about Sylvester trying to get a job up near the base, she thought, but I don't think she really does. She hasn't been acting like herself at all, and I know it's not because of her leg.

Joan watched out the window as they rode along the pike, watching groups of little houses placed here and there along the way, some facing the road, others facing each other. With all of them zipping by, it was hard to play the imagine game. It had been a hobby of hers to imagine who lived inside, how many people, what they did, and what their names were. Since she couldn't possibly know any of that, it was fun to give them dramatic or comical names, like Doolittle Longhorn and his wife Laura May, or Aurelia and Juanita, the Pacavera sisters. There was one house on the bus route that stood alone. Joan imagined that it was inhabited by one old lady and her 27 cats. She giggled, remembering some of her made up names of the cats, Packy, Wooly, Wonder Face, Ralph.

Then she looked down at her gloved hands, thought quickly of her handsome fiancé, and felt a pang of missing him. He's even further away than Sylvester, she thought. I'm not upset. I know he had to go and visit his family. I would expect that. And with Sylvester being gone to a job, surely Annie understands that. Maybe there's another reason that he left. Maybe Annie knows something about Sylvester's leaving that I don't know.

In the twilight that evening as Joan walked down her block, she decided it was time to be a little more direct with Annie. After all, she was her best friend, wasn't she? If there was something to tell, and something to hear, then they should be telling and hearing about it.

Inside the house, she put away her coat and thought about dinner. "I'm hungry!" she said out loud.

As if by magic, when she stepped into the kitchen, there on the table sat a beautiful date & nut tea ring! It was covered with wax paper and a little note in Annie's handwriting that said, "Try me, I'm delicious!" and below that, "Joanie, I'll be a little later today, I got a late start. See you around 6:30, Annie."

"Well, I'll have a piece right now, then!" said Joan chuckling. She set the kettle on the heat. "Or as soon as this water boils."

By the time Annie got in, their vegetable dinner was ready, but this time with the promise of a nice dessert. "Thanks for the tea ring!" Joan said. "I've already had some. Did your mom send it over?" Annie's family owned a very successful Atlantic City bakery, a fact that often gave Annie and Joan special privileges in the treats department.

"No, Margaret," Annie said. "I saw her at lunch time, and she mentioned it then. I had some, too. It's good isn't it?"

Margaret was a young woman whom Annie knew from working at the church. Annie's shop was to the back of the church, recently reconstructed to be separate from the church building, but somehow still connected to it. Margaret was the church secretary and very efficient.

"Yes, very," said Joan. "Wow, lunch with Margaret, huh?"

"No, I didn't have lunch with her. I just saw her then. But I told her to drop by sometime. We really haven't seen her much since Christmas."

"That's true."

"She's going to make some great cook, huh?" Annie said, hanging up her coat.

"You seem a little perkier today," Joan said. "It's nice to see."

"Well, some days I guess it just gets to me," Annie said.

"What does?"

"Just being separated and all, you know, from Sylvester."

"Oh believe me, I do! But it's not like he's that far away. It's only an hour's drive."

Annie hid her expression by turning to the stove and checking the casserole. "Oh this looks good. Yeah, just an hour away, you're right," she said ambiguously.

"And gosh, Dick's four hours away," Joan said. "I guess we're old maids again!" She laughed.

"Oh gosh Joan, do you have to be so dramatic?"

"Well, no—dramatic? Who's the one being dramatic and moody just because her fiancé is trying to find some work?"

"Dramatic and moody? I've been trying to spare you hearing my whining about things. Some people don't constantly talk about their personal feelings all the time."

"It might do you good to talk about personal feelings some of the time," Joan said. "It seems like you never do that anymore, at least not with me."

Just then she thought she heard Annie draw in her breath. But right as she started to soften, and ask her what was wrong, someone knocked on the door.

"Now who's here right at dinner time? I know it can't be Mrs. St. John," Joan said on her way to answer it.

She opened the door to find Margaret.

"Hello, Joan," she said. "I realize it's dinner time, but I wonder if I could have a quick word with Annie." She let herself in and stood expectantly inside.

Joan went back toward the kitchen, turned to Annie and called out, "Your new best friend is here!" and then continued on to her room to sit and brood.

Chapter Four

It was Joan's heart that was on Dick Thimble's mind as he went through his belongings in the home in which he'd grown up. He wondered how she was, what it was like for a young lady trudging out into the winter morning, needing to earn enough to pay her bills and keep fed. He hated being so far away, thinking of her fending for herself.

She was such a delicate thing, he thought, remembering holding her when they danced. Boy, we're a perfect match on the dance floor, he thought. She just about floats.

He sighed. What kind of security can I give her? Maybe when I was still Master Sergeant, but now. I've gotta figure out something. I've already asked her to marry me. And if I don't manage a plan in a hurry, I have to let her out of her promise.

That thought was like a sword in his heart. There was no option. He could not let her get away, so the only answer was to get a job, a career happening, and move ahead so the two of them could make plans.

Plans were a coveted concept, a treasure that only recently had fallen within his reach. In the military, all plans had been the property of his commanding officer. His was to complete objectives, manage his men the best he could, and bring about the best resolutions to what confronted him.

Today, he could decide where he would be the next day. Ironically, although the freedom to decide was his, he was no longer provided for. "It's one thing or the other," he said to himself, smiling as he remembered his father's words. "All in all, I'd rather have the freedom to decide, though."

His father had left the world while he was in France, struggling to survive a bullet wound, but sometimes Dick could still feel his presence. Their very close friendship had made the news of his loss extremely painful at the time, but now that he had come beyond it, he enjoyed the benefits of having his father's memory and expressions still so present in his mind. They brought him more joy than he had known possible. In fact, he had never heard of relationships running on after one person died, but somehow it still felt like his dad was around.

He thought of Bob, his good and close friend before, during, and now after their days in the service. Bob had suffered, Dick thought. Having his leg nearly wrenched off at the knee by the daggone machine gunner. I wish I'd have seen that sniper hiding in the dugout. I was the leader, I should have spotted him.

They were thoughts Dick would have many times again before eventually letting them come to rest. But they brought to mind memories of all of the service men in the days after Christmas, getting together and making a pact.

There had been six of them, if you counted Bobby back in Philadelphia. Dick remembered the tall, dark Sylvester, whom they all called "Sly" and the buddy he talked about name Bobby. Sly seemed to be a pretty good guy, and he had had the idea of all the fellows getting together in the first place.

Bob had said sure, why not? And Dick went along. He had enjoyed getting to know Harry, Sly and Bobby's captain, who was older and probably wiser, but still full of fun, Dick thought. And then there was Henry, also connected with Sly and Bobby but in much the same way he and Bob were connected — a lifesaving situation. Apparently, Henry had saved Sly's life, and then Sly and Bobby had saved Henry's life!

Dick chuckled. Reads like a military soap opera, he thought, but it was true. And with the way things had happened with he and Bob, there was no doubt they had the same deep brotherhood between them.

That had prompted Sly to seek them all out, he thought. It was that very Christmas night that Sly had proposed the idea, and everyone, to a man, said yes. They would meet back there every year, no matter what was going on, unless they were imprisoned somewhere — or worse — and share a drink to their camaraderie and survival.

But there was more. They would also act as a brotherhood. If one were in trouble, the others would offer what they could to help him out. Dick thought about the talks he had with his father about the first War, and how a close band of men would have brought some true peace and comfort to him.

Sly had spoken about that, how the men returning from the first big War had suffered from being unemployed and hungry, injured and unable to work, felt tossed aside and useless because of their lack of education. And he talked about how his father had known that despair and encouraged him to attend college so that it wouldn't happen to him.

That had struck a chord with Dick. And the government was making it possible for the smarter GIs to go to college, and those that didn't could use a sum of money for something else, a home, a business, whatever they felt would best help them. The home sounded nice, but Dick wanted more education. He admired the way Sly carried himself, and the confidence he seemed to feel. I want that, too, Dick said to himself. I know I was respected in my role as Master Sergeant, and I'm proud of that. But I want to have that kind of self-respect, feel that kind of command of myself.

In a very different way, Annie was also thinking about Sly. Joan had retired for the night, in kind of a snit, Annie thought. But she didn't feel like investigating Joan's troubles that night. After all, Joan was deliriously happy and would have no understanding of what Annie was going through, she thought, and she would have to spell it all out. No thanks!

She sat on her large easy chair in the corner of the room where she liked to sit and read, while sipping coffee. She leaned back into the soft comfort of it, remembering Sly's strong arms and gentle laugh. The one night had been so magical.

She and Sly had met up with Sly's friend Bobby and his brand new wife, Debbie. They were taking their honeymoon in Atlantic City. The four of them had talked and laughed, danced at the Boardwalk Ballroom and found beautiful romance, bundled up, walking in couples in the darkness of the well-patrolled boardwalk. As they stood together, staring out at the ocean, an officer from Civil Defense tapped Sylvester on the shoulder.

"Excuse me, what do you kids think you're doing out here?" he asked.

Sylvester had turned, laughing, and said, "Kids? You mean us?"

"To us, you're kids," said the man, who looked to be about 60 years old. "Get on inside to the dance now, this part of the boardwalk is only for our men in uniform."

Sylvester caught Bobby's eye, both of them struggling to control themselves.

"Yeah, that's how he got that bum leg, Buddy," said Bobby, all fired up. "Sitting around playing soldier in a Civil Defense outfit."

"It's okay, Bobby."

"We just got home after living in a hell hole for months, and yeah in uniforms, so I will thank you to show a little respect."

"I'm sorry boys, I didn't mean any offense," said the man. "I see a couple fellows out here making time with beautiful women, I just figured—"

"Don't figuah!" said Bobby, pointing his finger in the air. And he walked toward the hall with Debbie, calling "Come on, Sly," over his shoulder.

The officer put out his hands. "I didn't mean any offense. You guys are the best."

"No offense," said Sylvester. "Don't worry about it. Come on, Doll." He smiled mischievously at Annie. "We don't want Bobby to blow a gasket."

Despite his hot temper, Bobby did make a good impression on Annie, who secretly admired the fiery types. Although, as she told Sly, she wouldn't want to be all that close to someone like that. She also liked Bobby's new wife, Debbie, who seemed to be a perfect match for him.

"I have to say, I have definitely heard a lot about you!" she said to Bobby, shaking his hand, "But it's you I want to know more about," she said to Debbie laughing. "We have to work together to figure these fellows out!"

Debbie was short of stature but not on laughter or kindness. Annie took a liking to her as soon as they met. They hadn't had much more than a few minutes in the ladies' room to really talk, but she knew Debbie was "good people," as her mother used to say. No airs, down to earth, and Bobby loved her. That was good enough for Annie anyway.

Debbie already liked Annie because Annie was Sly's girl, and Sly had saved Bobby's life. But she liked her plenty whether all of that were true or not, and she hoped that time would bring them all closer.

"It's gonna be hard, them doing all the spy stuff, huh?" Debbie had said as they left the ladies room.

"Huh?" Annie said. "What?"

But Debbie had spotted Bobby just outside, and they were locked in an embrace in seconds. Annie thought surely Debbie was talking about something that had happened before. Maybe she meant "supply" as in the job that Sly was checking out up north. Not "spy." At that point, Annie hadn't given it another thought.

In fact, the evening had been extremely memorable. After Bobby and Debbie returned to their room, Sly and Annie took the long walk to the bus stop and relished in the long-awaited time together, laughing, hugging, walking arm-in-arm and feeling fully alive for the first time in years.

When they arrived at Helen's House where Annie was staying then, it was quiet so they sat in the kitchen and had tea.

"Tell me how you envision the future, Annie, our future," asked Sly.

"Our future?" Annie drew in her breath. She wondered if she would ever think of the future with Sylvester without feeling the large wings of butterflies within. She smiled, "Well, Honey, I honestly see us one day having that house, you can't see it now, with the blackout, but there's one on the corner of Edison, about a block and a half down, with the most beautiful front porch and garden. I don't think it's occupied right now because the Fogels passed away and they didn't have any children. But we sure would!"

"How many?" Sly asked smiling, squeezing her hand.

"I don't know, I think at least two maybe four."

"Only four?"

Annie laughed. "How many do you want? Ten?"

"Ten's good," he said. "Nice round number."

"That might be a few too many for me!" Annie laughed.

"We'll just take whatever God gives us," said Sly. "That okay with you?"

"That's great with me," Annie said.

She remembered the kiss that followed that, and her laughter, saying, "Hold on Honey, we're not married yet!"

It was all such a sweet memory. Annie couldn't let go of it, but somehow still, it felt stolen. It wasn't until the next day that her heart began to break.

On that Saturday morning, Bobby had dropped Debbie off at the beauty parlor. Annie and Joan were heading out to the grocery store to see if they could get their sugar rations filled. Bernice had said she was hoping to get supplies in that day and that they should come early. Bobby and Sly were having coffee in the kitchen when they left.

They'd gotten halfway down the block when Annie remembered that she had left her coin purse on her dresser. "You go ahead, Joanie, I'll meet you at the store. No sense in your standing around waiting."

"I will, if that's all right because I want to get in line—I'll hold your place."

"Yeah, that's good. I'll hurry."

But as Annie opened the door, she heard the men talking excitedly. Not necessarily arguing but so involved that they did not hear the door open.

Bobby was saying, "The war ain't over, Sly. Ain't no sense in us trying to act like a couple of school boys. I say we take it."

"I don't know," Sly had answered, "Do you think it'll be good pay? That's a long haul from here."

"Oh you ain't gonna be able to drive it, you'll have to relocate," Bobby said. "This is serious stuff. They got what they're calling operatives all around. We gotta keep it away from here. Debbie ain't coming."

"You just got married!"

"I know it, and she knows it. She gets it. She's pretty tough you know, city gal. She don't even want to move from Philly. She'll stay with her family and we'll have weekends, you know. I ain't goin' longer 'an a week," Bobby said lowering his voice.

"All right, all right," Sly said.

Annie closed the door and hurried after Joan down the sidewalk without getting her coin purse. She could make up an excuse, she thought. But her mind was swimming, her stomach was turning, and her heart was breaking.

That day, she could not bring herself to share what she had heard with Joan. And she felt horrible about not sharing it with Sylvester, but she felt as if she had been spying on them, listening there without letting them know she was there, which was hard to admit. And on top of that, wouldn't it be better if he came to her and told her personally? After all, they were engaged. Shouldn't he take that responsibility?

It wasn't that much longer before Sly came to her and explained that he was going to try to go for a job about an hour away. "I need to work," he had said, but without mentioning anything about it being dangerous or part of the war or anything.

"I understand that," Annie had said, knowing how ambiguous she was being. He deserved it, she thought.

But after he had left that day, she felt guilty and decided to tell him what she'd heard and ask him not to go into dangerous, secret agent type stuff. She would remind him that he was home, the war for him was over.

But when they next met, he simply announced that he was going to go up to somewhere near Wrightstown and see if he could get a job.

"Why can't you work here?" Annie asked. "Maybe in Atlantic City, in shipping or something?"

"Annie, I'm trained in some things and I feel like I should work in my field," he said.

Annie had not been angry; instead she became very sad, believing that he was not as serious as she was, and was willing to go far away from her to take a "spy" kind of job rather than stay and work somewhere here or nearby. Besides all that, with only those few words from Debbie and from eavesdropping on them that time in the kitchen, she feared for Sly's safety. Even back home, she thought bitterly, he'd prefer to leave her and run off and play spies.

That night in her room, Annie stood at the window, defiantly opening the shade to look at the stars. They were softly screened back with a milky cloud cover, but she could still see them.

"There's nothing like winter stars," she said softly to herself.

Then, remembering an earlier experience with a Civil Defense Officer, she quickly withdrew, lowering the shade back down, and heading for the kitchen.

"If all else fails," she said to herself, "hot tea and sweets." She took out Margaret's tea ring and cut herself a generous slice.

Chapter Five

"This ain't bad," Bobby said nodding, walking the perimeter of the room Sly had rented. "I got a sink, too, and mirror and stuff. Where do you put your snacks?"

"Snacks?"

"You know, salamis and stuff."

"I don't have any. They got breakfast at 8:00 in the morning, I just wait 'til then."

"Oh man I can't go the whole night without nothing to eat. I'd starve! You come ovah my place, I'll show you a sangwich."

Sly smiled remembering how Bobby's food talk had gotten them through tough times in combat. "You're the expert," he said. "And now you got, what, couple hundred bucks left from your wedding?"

"Shoot, couple hundred bucks. Debbie's got a hold of that money, every last penny. I had to apply for a loan to get my rent for here."

Sly laughed. "Already on a budget, huh?"

"Yeah, she's got some idea that we're going to have a house in two years. I don't see it, but she might as well dream."

"She could be right," Sly said, and plopped on the bed. "Listen, speaking of the women, I didn't exactly tell Annie about this opportunity. I left it with her and everybody that I was just coming up here to look at a job possibility."

"What'd you do that for?" Bobby asked, looking offended.

"Well, I wasn't embarrassed about it, if that's what you think."

"Oh, okay, well what's the deal?"

"It's not a civilian oriented job. It's more Intelligence than civilian. And I know she worries that I'll be taking off again."

Bobby gave him a knowing look. "Well . . . you know, you might. They didn't guarantee we'd stay here on base the whole time."

Sly looked at his shoes. "I know it. And I love the idea of this job and all, but the main reason I took it has to do with what you and Debbie were talking about."

"Me and Debbie?"

"Yeah, the house and all. I found out the house Annie wants. Man, I don't have that kind of money. And I wouldn't earn it in a low-level civi job either. With this job, I figure in six months, a year, I'll have a good down payment, and we can take it from there."

"You gonna finish college?"

"Oh yeah."

"'Cause you know, I finished, and I figure once we're done here, or the war comes out, whichever happens first, we're college men. We can afford to look around. They got trains into Philly from where you live, you could work there and make a bundle."

Sly nodded. "Yeah. I gotta get over to New Brunswick and finish out that class. I got one class and a couple of final exams they said they'd hold, then I'm done."

"That's the way to go. But Sly, you know, you gotta level with Annie."

"Well if we have to go over to It'ly again, she's gonna figure it out pretty fast."

"Is that the way you want her to find out?"

"No."

"I told Debbie, look Babe, I gotta do this. You want a house? I gotta do this. Then we'll figure out where I go from there. She goes, but I'll miss you! I told her, good!" He laughed.

"I worry that what I'm doing goes against what I told her before, that I was home, and I was safe."

"Well you were, then."

"Yeah. I know I gotta do this. And I know I gotta tell her." He sighed. "So what kind of sangwich would you have put together with them two hundred bucks?"

"Oh man!" said Bobby. "Start with the bread, that downtown Philly bread—a loaf maybe a mile long. No not that long, maybe a block. Yeah, and you slop on that sauce, what's it called?"

"Mustard? Ketchup?"

"No, no, that sauce, kind of like gravy, what do they call it?"

"You mean the marinara?"

"Yeah, yeah, and you get a nice pile of chicken cutlets, fried up thin and crisp, and you top 'em with the provolone—that's how you start it off, right?"

"Yeah, so far so good."

"Then you gotta get some ripe tomatoes. Nice red ones and slice them up, lay 'em on there with the lettuce, romaine if you got it. And then—"

"Okay, okay, you're making me hungry. Let's go out. They got a deli we can walk to, my treat."

"Well that was easy!"

At about the same time, Harry was thinking about having lunch. "What do we got for lunch?" he asked Helen, as he screwed the face of the utensil drawer back onto the box. "You sure get good use out of this, by the way."

"I didn't do anything to it," Helen said defensively. "That thing sticks almost every time I try to open it. I might just move the utensils to another drawer and store something else in there."

"Like what?"

"Oh, I don't know. Popsicle sticks. Extra ice cube trays."

"How about swizzle sticks and ballet shoes?"

"No, the ballet shoes would create an unappetizing aroma. At least if they were yours, they would."

Harry faked offense. "All right, now you're going to get it!" he said throwing the screwdriver and giving chase.

Helen gave a little surprised scream and tried to take off but he caught her by the elbow and pulled her close.

"I'm still pretty spry, Mrs. Ashenbach."

"You are that," Helen answered. "But I thought you were looking for lunch."

"It's almost Valentine's Day. Maybe I want dessert first."

Helen laughed. "Only if you want cold vegetable soup and cold corn muffins."

Harry dropped her arms and ran to the stove. "We got vegetable soup! Oh boy!"

Helen got out the bowls and spoons. "Grab me a couple of napkins out of the towel drawer," she said, "Fickle Fred."

"Oh not Fickle, just putting first things first," he said with a grin.

"That's what you think," Helen said. "I've got my priorities, too."

Harry set the napkins on the kitchen table and sat down. "Oh yeah? What have you got coming up?"

"Well, I think we'd better get something figured out, you and I," Helen said a little sternly.

"Figured out? I thought we were doing pretty good, woman," Harry chuckled.

"No complaints," Helen said, "except that I suspect there is a secret, and while I can tolerate some job secrets, I don't like what it's doing to Annie."

Harry marveled at his wife. There could be bombs blasting through the neighborhood and combat men storming the house, grenades going off, and people yelling and screaming all over the place, and if one of those people was keeping a secret, she'd know who it was.

He sighed. "All right," he said.

"Well, tell me," Helen said.

"Can I have my lunch first?"

"I guess so." She ladled out a large bowl of vegetable soup made with the beef broth she'd frozen back in November. Garlic had been plentiful, and it went a long way toward enriching her dishes, especially soups and gravies.

She brought a basket of corn muffins to the table, still hot from the oven, knowing that Harry was good for at least 4.

"Oh I love these," he said as he filled his bread & butter plate.

"I know it. It's nice to see you eat. It's just nice to see you, period."

He squeezed her elbow. "Forever grateful."

She said down. "Yes," she said smiling at him. "Say grace?"

After they'd eaten and the dishes were cleared away, and the drawer put back together, Helen said, "It's been a long couple of years, Honey, and I've gotten to know these girls very well. We were like a lifeline to each other while you were all away. We went through panics and fears, our little joys at getting letters, and long, lonely waiting. We shared it all. I hate to see Annie suffering over the confusion about this move by Sylvester. I know how he feels about her. And who in his right mind would take some run of the mill job where he'd have to move an hour away and see her only occasionally? Why? What is going on?"

"I really feel Sylvester should be the one to say," Harry started out, "but there's no reason it has to stay secret between you and me."

"Okay."

"Well the boys, and I mean Sly and Bobby, you know, they were inseparable. They've got a history I don't want to spell out to you but they been through some stuff that will keep them bound together for the rest of their lives."

"It's good. I think it's the boys who don't have a close sense of friendship that suffer more afterwards, coming home, getting adjusted, finding a job, that sort of thing," Helen said.

"Exactly right!" Harry said, standing up, walking to the window. "You've hit the nail on the head. These guys are used to working hard all day, every day. They want to keep working, and they want to provide for the women they love. Hell, Bobby's already married. There was no stopping them!" He laughed. "But aside from needing to be productive, and needing to be with their gals, they also need that challenge. You have to understand, Helen, these two guys were tops, I mean unbelievably helpful in the interrogation room. There were no tricks or meanness, but they had a way of getting information that we really needed. And it gave them a sense of pride and accomplishment."

"I understand all that, I mean I do as best as a civilian can," Helen said. "But don't you think Annie understands that? And what is the need to move away? What don't we know?"

"I think Annie is perfectly capable of managing the truth," Harry said. "It's Sly. He don't want to hurt her, worry her, and most of all, well. . ."

"Go on," Helen said, getting up and shoving him on the shoulder.

"Well, the position he's taken requires him to work six to 12 months, like it or not, and Helen, he might have to go back to Italy."

Helen sighed. "I was afraid it was something like that. Why would he risk getting injured again? Doesn't he realize the odds at this point?"

"Well, he does, but these intelligence positions—"

"Intelligence! Intelligence?"

"Well, I was getting to that. Yes, he's in the Intelligence sector. By tomorrow afternoon, he'll be trying his best, along with Bobby, to decode Nazi messages encoded in some sort of Italian protocol. They do it right there at Dix, but if need be, they'll travel overseas. It's civilian work of course, but it's a military job description. Those guys have got familiarity with a lot of the dialects now, and they're also familiar with the ways the enemy tries to communicate, angles he takes and where he hides information. That's why they were recruited. They're both ideal for the position. And Honey, it pays very well."

Helen shook her head and sighed again. "I understand it. I don't like it, but I understand it. It almost seems like it would be dangerous even here, in the States."

"Well," said Harry, fiddling with the window shade.

"Well?"

"There is a certain degree of danger. You have to understand, this War is being fought now with everything they got. We're giving it our all and we're actually winning, the way I see it. That's due in large part to our intelligence on the ground. There may be, and I'm not saying for certain, but I have heard rumors that there are operatives in and around the bases where the decoding takes place. So yes, there could be some incidents. Nothing like the danger we faced overseas, but there could be. . . problems."

Helen began to wash the dishes, her back to Harry. "Well I don't like any of it," she said. "And I think the sooner Annie knows, the better."

"I don't either, on the one hand. But if anyone tells Annie, Helen, it's got to be Sly."

About 180 miles away in Northwest Washington, D.C., Dick opened the mailbox and found a letter addressed to him among other things for his mother.

"Are you awake, Mom?" he called softly. She had taken to spending about an hour napping out of every two hours waking. He smiled, happy that she was happy. Her life had become a series of get togethers with her friends, church on Sundays, and easy reading and writing of letters.

It had been such a relief to find her in that condition. He hadn't known what to expect. Even when she took a little ill or felt her arthritis particularly, she still had friends come over and they shared memories and laughter.

Since she didn't answer, he left her letters on the kitchen table and put on the kettle to boil. One thing they had was plenty of tea. Every friend or neighbor seemed to know about her love of tea and as a result, she had probably the largest variety and the biggest stash of anyone in the Metropolitan area. He joked with her that she should open a shop.

He decided to scoop some Earl Gray and one precious lump of sugar into one of her china cups. She had collected china in her earlier years, as well as angel figurines. Now days she kept all of her angels on the shelves with the tea cups and it gave the kitchen a very welcoming feel. He carried the hot tea into his room to read his letter from Bob.

He feared the letter would report much the same trouble there that he was having in his hometown with respect to finding work. But things would get better. He was sure. They had to because he had no choice in the matter, and he knew God would provide him opportunities. He had gotten this far, and he knew that if he continued to persevere, one way or another, he would succeed.

Hey Buddy! it began, you couldn't have written at a better time. Dick's heart leapt. I'm about to get myself a place—it's small but I figure it'll do me until I get married. You can join me, and maybe take it over. But the best news is yet to come—listen to this. Good old Bernice, you remember, Joanie and Annie's friend? Well she's got that grocery store. Oh it's a nice place and all, but it's been kind of run into the ground. I worked on the books for the fellow who's managing it and tried to let him know how to maintain them a little better.

Anyway, Bernice says he wants to retire. I hadn't realized that before. She says she tried to learn the business, but just couldn't do that and try to learn nursing at the same time. She's got all kinds of plans, that gal, and the long and the short of it is, she wants me to manage! I was tickled pink! It's a living—just by itself. And of course I can still take on accounting clients like before. I'm over the moon buddy.

And here's another little piece of news you're gonna like. There's a place there for you—part time, but it'll be good enough to keep you in rent and rations until you get your money or decide what you want to do.

Aint it great, buddy? We're gonna be back in the same unit! I'm sure Joanie'll be thrilled too! Write me back, let me know what you want to do.

It didn't take Dick long to put pen to paper in response.

You bet that was great news! I couldn't have asked for anymore! And yes, if that offer stands, I'd very much like to share the digs you've found, now and of course after you move into your new home with your bride.

The job you offer is a godsend. I'm unsure of what I plan to do, but I'm set on getting into a career. I want to have a situation that was similar to my military position when I marry, so that I'm not just working but moving into a life that can benefit Joan and me. I've read several articles about the men from the last War and the struggles they've had because of either no jobs or low-paying jobs.

I think our college has helped us, but I want to maybe specialize in something. I'm still thinking about all of this, but this situation you offer is just primo and I thank you sincerely. I will be there as soon as I can, probably in a week or two. Please don't let Joan (or Laureen) know. I'd like to surprise her.

Dick mailed the letter that afternoon and began to pack what things he would need. His friend had given his spirits such a lift. He thought of Joan and how happy she would be.

He counted his money. Fifty-eight dollars and change. Maybe he would check the bus schedule. He hadn't taken a bus to the Jersey shore when he lived in Washington. He and Bob had always driven together.

Next he made a small supper of macaroni and cheese and brought up some jarred fruit from his mother's cellar. She woke up just as it was ready.

"That smells good," she said smiling as she toddled into the kitchen.

Mrs. Thimble's small features were framed in a gentle halo of soft white hair. Her eyes sparkled with interest. "What did you cook?"

"Macaroni and cheese, Mama," Dick said. "And I hope it's alright. I brought up some of last summer's peaches."

"Oh my yes," she answered, her voice quiet but not lacking in enthusiasm. "What a good combination."

As they ate, Dick explained his hopes and plans for the coming months. He worried that she would be disappointed, but he had his second surprise of the day.

"That's great news," she said. "I think it means we just might see grandchildren sooner! I could win the race with Mildred and Winnie both. Winnie thinks she's got the lead." She laughed lightly.

Dick hugged his tiny mother. "You're amazing, Mama," he said.

She patted his back, chuckling. "I certainly am," she said.

Chapter Six

Joan stepped off the evening bus from City and into the brisk February air. She drew in her breath as a cloud of exhaust billowed around her behind the ancient departing vehicle.

"Old rattletrap," she said between coughs.

On that night, Joan felt as if she were carrying 50-pound blocks of ice in her coat. Her bones ached and her nose seemed to be getting more sniffly as the day wore on.

It's got to be all this exhaust, she thought. It's making me sick. I need to move a little faster once I get off the bus. Oh, but today I'm so tired. I must not be getting enough sleep. Let's see, when did I hit the hay last night? I guess it was. . . She couldn't remember.

The sidewalk journey seemed long but she had no choice, so she trudged on, stopping to sneeze now and then, and rub her eyes.

Once inside, she immediately hung up her coat and ran to get into her warm pajamas and robe. Something told her to snuggle up with a book. But she knew there was nothing prepared for dinner.

Why is it always me who has to make dinner, she thought, when Annie lives here, too? She never makes anything. Temporarily forgetting about the treats Annie regularly brought to the house that no one else on the whole street was privy to, Joan began to feel resentful.

She slunk into the kitchen and turned on the stove for tea. For some reason, the element in the burner picked that very day not to work. Out of frustration and without thinking, Joan yanked the tea kettle off of the burner, instantly showering herself with cold water in the process.

"Oh!" she yelled, startled and angry at the same time. "Why don't they make these teakettles with better tops!" she demanded out loud and stomped back into her bedroom to change her pajamas.

Once inside, she found that she had only the bottom half of a spare set, and no top. She decided it would be better to be dry than to be coordinated, so she put on the pajama pants, and a t-shirt she found on her bed, and grabbing her robe returned to the kitchen.

Angrily she slammed the teakettle down on another burner, turned it on and saw the element begin to light up. Still in a snit, she spun around to go to the table, forgetting that there would be water on the floor. A split second before she thought it might be better to slow down, her feet went out from under her and the next thing she knew, she was in a heap on the floor, up against the cabinet.

It was there she sat, reconsidering her actions, when Annie came through the door, carrying a cakebox in

front of her. Approaching the table, Annie did not spot
Joan on the floor, and jumped into the air when she
heard her voice say, "It's not what it looks like."

Twisting her bad ankle, Annie nearly went down
on top of Joan, but instead grabbed the edge of the
table and held on. The table, not being weighted down
with anything other than a cotton centerpiece, was easy
prey, and obligingly lifted its hind legs and came down
right on top of Annie.

Still intent on identifying the voice, while holding
the table and being temporarily blinded by the
centerpiece dangling from the top of her head where it
slid, Annie said, "Where are you?"

"Behind you," came Joan's voice. "Gosh, Annie are
you okay?"

"Oh, there you are. What—yes, I'm okay—what are
you doing on the floor?"

"Same as you," Joan said, "just passing the time."

The two of them looked at each other for a second,
and then burst out laughing.

"What did I slip in?" Annie finally asked, trying to
get out from under the table. "Ouch!"

"My water," Joan said.

"Your. . . water? Ew! You don't mean. . ."

"No!" Joan giggled. "I mean I spilled water, which
is how I fell and then how you fell, and I guess if
Bernice had come in, how she would have fallen."

Annie started laughing. And then laughing harder.

"It's not that funny," said Joan, rubbing her right
hind quarter.

"No, not that," Annie said between breaths. "Why,
why are you wearing that shirt?"

"What shirt? My t-shirt?"

"That t-shirt!"

Joan tried to look down at it.

"You don't see that?" said Annie, struggling to stand up on her one good leg.

Joan looked to the left and gasped. "What is that?" she cried. "Am I bleeding?"

Annie giggled and sniffed, "No, no, you're okay, you're okay. Jeeze. Sit down, Joanie. It's jam. I had to use that to clean the counter real fast the other day and I didn't get a chance to wash it out."

"I must be pretty far gone not to notice I'm wearing a shirt with jam smeared on it." Joan threw a hand towel on to the floor to soak up the puddle before carefully pulling up the table and sitting down.

"No," Annie said, sitting down, "just worn out."

"Worn out? Me? From what?"

"You been back at work for a while now. You're not used to it full time, Joanie. It can really take a lot out of you, especially after you've been off for a while."

"Maybe. I ache all over. That's how I happened to fall. I was trying to make some tea and spilled the water on the floor, and it all went downhill from there."

"Now that we're back on our feet," Annie said, giggling, "I guess we'd better get something in the oven."

"I was just getting ready to make tea," Joan said. "I really don't feel that great. I'm freezing for one thing."

"Well go in there and sit down, I'll get the tea. The water's almost hot."

Joan followed her instructions and gratefully accepted a cup of hot tea from her limping friend after only a few minutes' wait. "Are you having some? Gosh Annie, I hope you didn't reinjure your leg."

"I'll be in in a minute. I want to throw something together for dinner. Don't worry about my ankle—I was just trying out a new walk."

Just then the door opened and Bernice charged in carrying a brown paper bag. "I'm still sneezing," she said.

"Close the door," Annie said. "You're too late. We finished our falling routine five minutes ago."

"Huh?"

"More like 10 minutes ago," Joan said, sipping her tea.

"Let me go out and come back in again," Bernice said heading for the door.

"Get in here," Annie said, grabbing her by the elbow. "You want some tea?"

"I'd love some. But I'm really feeling left out. How come you didn't wait for me to be part of the falling routine?"

"It's not your strong point," Annie said. "I've been falling pretty good lately. First there was the fire, then Sly knocks me over, and then today, I slipped in Joan's water."

"What?" said Bernice looking at Joan. "You didn't!"

"No, I didn't," said Joan making a face at Annie.

"It was genuine water," Annie said. "But it was Joan's."

"You know, sometimes when I come over here, I feel like there's the regular world, and then there's you guys' one."

"How long have you had that cold?" Annie asked, ignoring her statement.

"I must have gotten it just before we all got together at Helen's, on the weekend. It was windy on my way over and I could feel it cutting through my jacket."

"That's what I thought," said Annie. "I think you might have gotten carried away with generosity. Joan's got it now."

"Oh, Joanie, I'm so sorry!" Bernice said.

"I'm not sick," said Joan. "Nothing for you to be sorry about."

Bernice looked at Annie. "You can be pretty mean spirited."

"I think she's sick. She doesn't want to be, but I think she is."

"Well, I feel bad. I didn't mean to do that, Joanie."

"I'm not sick."

"How about if I tell you a story?"

"Tell her the one about the princess and the frog," Annie said, putting several eggs in the pan. "You're having dinner over."

"Okay. Oh, and here, I brought yous some ground meat and licorice."

"Oh!" said Joan. "You are wonderful! Licorice, let me see!"

"Wait 'til dinner, Joanie!" Annie whined from the kitchen.

"Okay, okay."

"What about the story now?" Annie asked.

"All right. Once there was a Princess who wanted to marry a handsome prince. She would hang around outside the castle, hoping to catch the eye of a passing prince. Well, bye and bye--why do they always say 'bye and bye,' this happened or that happened? What is that supposed to mean? Who are they saying goodbye to?" Bernice asked.

"What?" said Annie.

"By and by," said Joan. "Not bye and bye."

"What?" said Annie.

"You know, speaking of bye, if you are sick, and you will know tomorrow, I hate to say it but you will not be able to attend that St. Valentine's Day dance that you have been working so hard on."

Silence hung in the air.

"Well, I don't know what to say about that," Annie finally said.

"We've got our dresses," said Joan, "even if they are remakes from our old hostess gowns."

"Can I have some tea now?" Bernice asked.

"Yeah," said Annie, handing her a cup, "but you might well be responsible for this year's St. Valentine's Day disaster."

By the following Friday, it was clear that none of the three would be attending the dance. Joan's cold blossomed rapidly, keeping her out of work by Friday, and Annie quickly followed suit.

"This is depressing," she said as the three of them sat on the couch.

"Yeah," said Joan, "we're old maids again."

Annie bristled. "Great, Joanie. That helps a lot!"

Bernice and Joan exchanged glances.

"What do you mean, Annie?" Joan asked. "It was just a joke."

"I don't like that kind of joke, okay?" Annie fired back.

No one said anything for a few minutes, then Annie sniffed and wiped her eyes, not from the cold. "I'm sorry," she said. "I'm just not sure what to do. I think it's slowly making me crazy."

"Well what is it, Annie?" Joan said, although it sounded more like, "Waddisit Addie?"

"It's Sylvester," Annie said. "I don't want to bring everyone down." She sighed heavily. "But he's been up there a couple weeks now, trying to get a job, so he says, and I never hear anything."

"But he's written you letters," Joan said gently.

"Yeah, letters, about what it's like there, how cold it is, the lady who runs the rooming house, but nothing about when, Joanie. When?"

Joan looked down. "Oh, that," she said. "I know."

The girls had both declined to talk about the big "when." Joan had been sure that Dick would be back in a few days, but the days had turned to weeks, and then, too she hadn't received a letter in several days. Their "when" hadn't even been mentioned since Christmas.

"Yes, that. I guess we should be used to not receiving letters," she said trying to make light of it. "But I think, I can't help coming to the conclusion that, I just suspect that there's something more to Sylvester's story."

"Something more?" Bernice asked. "What do you mean? You're not back on that floozy in the floorboards thing again, are you?"

Annie and Bernice had to laugh. During those hard times only months before, with the men stationed in Europe, somehow Annie had come to the conclusion that Sylvester's failure to write was due to a liaison with another woman, or "floozy," as she had expressed it.

"No, I don't think it's that. But, well, maybe I shouldn't say. Now that I'm talking about it, it kind of sounds, I don't know, silly."

"You haven't talked about anything!" Bernice said, sitting back and crossing her legs. "What are you worried about?"

"Well, I thought I heard, you know his friend, Bobby?"

"No," said Bernice.

"No," said Joan.

"Well, he's the one he was friends with in combat."

Bernice started giggling. "He was friends with? You mean they went to coffee together?"

"Okay, they were buddies or however they say it," Annie said. "Shut up, Bernice. And his wife—he got married right away—his wife said something under her breath once about the spy stuff, I think that's what she said."

"Spy stuff?"

"Yeah, she said, like aren't you worried about them doing all that spy stuff?"

"What did Sylvester say?"

"Oh he wasn't there, and I couldn't ask her to go on because Bobby was there. But that night, I can't remember what happened, but we started talking about us and there was no hint of him going away to some far away job. We talked all about our lives together in the future. Then, next thing I know, he's going to see about a job over an hour away!"

"Well that's probably why he wanted the job," Joan said. "He was thinking about the future and all."

"There's jobs here," said Annie. "So many that they got women working 'em."

"Yeah," said Bernice nodding. "That's true."

Joan and Bernice tried moving the conversation away from the subject, not really having a good answer, and eventually Bernice was able to clown them into forgetting about their absent boyfriends. But on the night of the Valentine's Day Dance, both girls were particularly glum.

"Sick and dateless," said Joan. "I bet old redhead Gloria would love to see me stuck at home tonight."

"Old redhead Gloria would be lucky to have a date herself," Annie said.

"Isn't she going with the fellow from Kresge's or something?" Bernice asked.

"I'm not sure if that's still on," Joan said. "After her friendliness at Midnight Mass, I thought she was turning over a new leaf. But that might not be the case."

"It's hard to change," Annie said. "The dance must be just about over now. I bet it was beautiful."

"Yeah, but honestly, wouldn't you rather be at home sick with a cold than standing around during a dance with no date?" Joan asked.

"I might rather be here whether I had a date or not," Annie said defiantly.

"Sure, you say that now," Bernice chuckled.

Just then, they heard a tap on the door. "Don't get up," Helen said, coming in the door. "I just thought I'd drop by and bring you these things. I'm so sorry you all got sick and couldn't go. But I've got a little pack of some of the foods we had. These little cheesey nut balls are very good!"

"Helen, you're a lifesaver," Annie said. "You should be home and cozy with Harry. He's going to be looking for you!"

"He's waiting for me outside," Helen said, "but he wants to smoke his cigar, so he's just sitting out there on the steps. He's happy, and we can have a few minutes anyway."

"Was it pretty, Helen, at the dance, I mean?" Joan asked.

"Yes, very nice. There weren't quite enough decorations to make it seem like a ballroom and not a church hall, but it was nice. The band was lively and I think the few men who were there, and the soldiers from Atlantic City really appreciated the benefit aspect of it."

"Did you dance?" Annie asked.

"Oh yes, I did the Watusi, and the jitterbug," Helen laughed. "We did dance a little, just like this." And she swung her ample posterior to and fro in an exaggerated manner, stepping out and around the room, making the girls laugh.

"I'm glad I didn't go," Joan laughed. "I sure don't know that dance!"

"You know who was there, I saw Bob and Laureen, and Margaret, with her Elwood. They're such a cute couple. I know Margaret has some quirkiness, but she deserves happiness like anyone else."

"Definitely," said Bernice.

"That's funny, coming from the evil woman who stole her baker," Joan giggled.

It wasn't true, and never had been true, but once Margaret had a thing in her head, she had no capacity to get it back out. She still bore Bernice ill will, even though Bernice never did a single thing, and went out of her way to be extra kind to Margaret.

"No, I mean it," said Bernice. "I'm happy that she and Elwood found each other. What do you want to bet they get married before anybody else? Wouldn't that be a hoot?"

"Yeah, a hoot and a half," said Annie. "Shut up Bernice."

"Oh, sorry," Bernice said.

"Listen," Helen said, "part of the reason I'm here is to bring you up to date on something. I guess you can all hear, since it's going to come up sooner or later."

Everyone leaned forward as if they were getting together to make plans for a raid.

But just then the phone rang. It was so late, and the room had become so still that it startled everyone.

"It can't be Sylvester," Annie said. "They got no phone."

"Answer it," said Joan.

Annie went to the phone and a few seconds later, she mouthed, "It's Sylvester!"

"It's Sylvester!" said Joan.

"Oh thank Heavens," said Helen. "I'm off the hook. I've got to go. He'll tell her. Harry told him to."

"Well so who's going to tell us?" Bernice said.

Helen smiled. "I don't know, nosey. Hopefully somebody will. You ladies enjoy your night. Hope you like the goodies!"

"Thanks Helen!" Joan called as Helen went out the door.

After the three-minute call was over, Annie grabbed a cup of tea and sat down with them. "You guys are not going to believe this," she said.

Chapter Seven

"Well don't leave us in suspense, Annie!" Bernice said. "What did he say? What's going on?"

"Where's Helen?" Annie asked.

"She said she was off the hook and just about ran out the door!" Joan giggled. "It must be something juicy."

"Ahhh," Annie said, as she slumped back against the couch pillows, putting her sore leg on a pillow. "I can breathe again!"

Joan picked up a pillow and Annie's foot and sat down with them on her lap. Bernice pulled up a chair. They knew Annie. She loved to dramatize the moment.

But they were getting a little impatient.

"Spill!"

Annie laughed. "He's got a job, just a job—no floozy, no signing back into the Army—"

"Did you think that's what he was doing?" Joan asked.

"I didn't know what he was doing," Annie said. "He was so secretive, I thought gosh, maybe he's gotten bored with life already and he's thinking about reenlisting."

"That ain't all you thought," Bernice said.

"You're right about that," Annie said. "I'm so ashamed of myself. But what was I supposed to think? Going off like that, over an hour's drive away, just hoping to get some job?"

"There's not much for them around here other than unskilled jobs right now. That might be the problem," Joan said. "I heard someone say the other day at work that they have to go where the work is. Gosh, I hope Dick doesn't think he has to stay in Washington!"

"One tragedy at a time, please," said Bernice.

Joan giggled nervously.

"And the reason it's been so long," Annie explained, is they had to go through some kind of security period. They couldn't make phone calls out or even receive them."

"Or write letters?" Joan asked.

"Their letters were monitored, like in the Army."

"Who's 'they?'"

"I guess he meant him and Bobby."

Bernice was skeptical. "Him and Bobby? Don't they already have security clearance? From being the interrogators and all?"

"I guess this was a different kind."

"Or maybe a different level," Joan added. "I heard they have levels, like secret, and very secret, that kind of thing."

"Yeah, I've heard of top secret, that kind of thing, but if this is just a job. . ." Bernice's voice trailed off.

Annie sighed.

"You're getting her all upset again, Bern," Joan said.

"I'm just curious," Bernice said. "Sylvester doesn't seem like the type to lie, so I'm curious what kind of job he or they have. It sounds pretty heavy duty."

Annie was quiet, staring intently at the floor. Everything he had said sounded genuine. Especially the part about getting impatient to set a date. But she knew the girls were right, even if they didn't say it. Something about this job, this mysterious job, was fishy.

In the first place, why on earth would Bobby come? They have more work in Philadelphia than anywhere for miles around. And didn't Sly say that Bobby had graduated college? Why did he need to go to a job where you had to apply and go through some sort of sequestering without communication?

On the other hand, she loved Sylvester and she knew he loved her. But would he tell her a lie? Or possibly would he maybe tell her just the part of the story that he wanted her to hear and leave out the rest?

Impossible.

"I know my fiancé," Annie said. "And if he says that's the way it is, that's the way it is."

"Okay," said Bernice. "I know you know him best."

Joan caught Bernice's eye, and shrugged.

At that same time, in a tiny diner down the street from their rooming house, Sylvester and Bobby sat having pot roast and mashed potatoes.

"I don't know how they get a hold of this stuff," Bobby said, "but I'm sure glad they do."

"Probably their own beef," Sylvester said.

"Man, that'd be hard. Gettin' up in the morning, looking one of your little cows in the eye and going, 'Okay, buddy, today it's you on the choppin' block.'"

"Jeeze, Bobby! You gotta do that while I'm eatin'?"

"Hey, sorry. Anyway, did you tell her?"

"Huh?"

"Yeah huh, you know what I mean. Did ya tell Annie what we been up to?"

"Well, I told her I got a job, it took a while, and we had to go through a security kind of period."

"Well, all that's true," Bobby said. "And what about the nature of the job, the field work, and possible travel?"

"Look, what's the point of getting her all upset?" Sylvester said. "She's happy now. She knows where I am, she knows we'll be able to start making plans soon."

"You hope."

"What?"

"You hope. What if they decide you're the one they want on that ship outta here next month?"

"Hell no it ain't gonna be me. I just got here."

"That don't mean nothin'," Bobby said, "you heard that guy at the orientation. He said anybody's liable to get called. It's some kinda lottery or something. It very well could turn out to be you. Then how are you going to explain things?"

Sly put down his fork and looked Bobby in the eye. "What are you, the voice of doom?"

"No, man, I just seen it before. You know, the guy lies, or holds out on the girl and the whammo, it's over. Curtains. And the guy feels so bad he starts drinkin' or some'n."

"And what does the girl do in this cheerful scenario of yours?"

"The girl? Oh, she starts eatin', you know, hamburgers and doughnuts, boxes of chocolate, next thing you know, she's three hundred pounds, and even if she let the guy back into her life, he's not so sure about things anymore."

Sylvester chuckled. "Can you see my Annie at three hundred pounds?"

"Hey it can happen. Mark my words, I seen it."

Sylvester went back to eating. "Yeah, I know you're right. But I gotta do this, Bobby, or there ain't no pretty house, no nice wedding. And if she knows, she'll, well she'll think I'm doing it because I still want to be in the action."

"And that's no way true, right?" Bobby said, chuckling.

"Well," Sylvester said. "Yeah."

They both laughed.

"Man, you're right. I gotta figure this out," Sylvester said. "Meanwhile, I want to finish up these mashed potatoes and my serving of Ol' Bessie."

At Sunday Mass next morning, Joan struggled between praying for herself, and wishing she didn't have to. Understanding was so tough. Even the word, *understanding*; it was how she felt compelled to feel. Standing under this out of balance situation, worrying that it was going to fall on top of her. She smiled in spite of herself. Having things fall on top of her was more Annie's department.

She had to stay strong, stay broadminded as her mother used to say. Of course, the men at work had had a field day with that in the back office. Broad minded, they'd say, accenting the first part of the word. But it was important to keep heart and mind

open. After all, what had just happened with Annie
and Sylvester? He was also incommunicado for a few
weeks, then all of the sudden, everything's fine. She
pushed Bernice's observations out of her mind.
Everything would be with Annie and Sly. It was
always meant to be, and it would be.

And that's how things would work out with Dick.
She didn't know where he was, or when she'd see him
again, but she knew she would, and that's when they
could start making their plans and getting on with life.

Just then she felt a gentle nudge at her shoulder.
She looked over to see the usher holding the collection
basket. Annie nudged her from the other side, covering
her mouth. Joan frantically rummaged through her
pocketbook looking for the little white envelope with
her offering.

"Joan!" Annie hissed.

"What?" Joan whispered. "I'm trying to find the
collection."

"It's in your lap!"

"Oh! Thank you." She tossed it into the basket and
the usher gave an appreciative nod and moved on.

What if I didn't have anything today, Joan
wondered, looking at Annie. That would have been
embarrassing.

"He saw it on your lap," Annie whispered, reading
her mind.

"Oh."

As the two of them walked home, Joan avoided the
subject of missing fiancés and instead asked Annie
what she thought might be a nice Sunday dinner,
provided they could find it in their kitchen.

"I'm really in the mood for spaghetti," Annie said. "It's still pretty cold out, although the wind is giving us a break today. And it's such a nice Sunday meal. Maybe we go over my folks' house."

"That's nice," Joan said, "but I feel like sticking close to home—"

"Don't I know it!" Annie said. "You're waiting for that telephone call!"

Joan sighed. There was no hiding things from her best friend. She and Annie had weathered some of the darkest days in their lives. Today was just a nice Sunday, though, there was some sun shining through, and they were going to make a nice dinner, and be grateful for that.

Nevertheless, Joan was careful to sit near the phone when she picked up her crochet work.

"You're smart to work on that this time of year. By the time next winter comes around, you'll have lots of nice afghans," Annie said, picking up a magazine.

"We need some, too!" Joan said. "I love this soft green. I went crazy buying up the yarn back when I worked at Kresge's. Everyone thought I was nuts. They were buying the blouses and jumpers. Of course they could use more of their paychecks. But now I'm so glad I did that. Gold and green will be a warm color combination, don't you think?"

"I love it," said Annie. "And I never would have thought of it."

Joan smiled and started in on the row of green double crochet when someone tapped on the door. "Did you hear that?"

"Yeah, sounds like someone's at the door," Annie said. "You want me to check?"

"I'll go," Joan said. "You stay put, read your magazine."

Despite her thoughts and wishes all morning, it was really the last thing on her mind that she would open the door that morning and find the tall and handsome Dick Thimble in his Sunday best. "Hello! Good morning!" he said smiling. "I'm glad to see I found the right house!"

Joan lost her breath for a few seconds, and when she caught hold of it again, she said, "You're here."

Dick smiled. "I would not even venture any opposition to that."

Joan heard a giggle from behind her. "Ask him in," Annie urged gently from the kitchen, knowing Joan's tendency to get flustered.

"Oh yes, come in. Dick! I'm so happy to see you!" she said, throwing her arms around him as if suddenly realizing that he wasn't a cartoon or the Fuller Brush man.

He returned her embrace, drawing in the scent of her hair and her light floral cologne.

"Coffee?" called Annie. "But if so, we really should have it inside."

Dick laughed, and releasing Joan, put an arm around her shoulder and walked inside with her. He set his hat down and followed Joan into the kitchen.

"Let me take your coat," she said, smiling. "It's just so good to see you!"

"I can't tell you how happy I am to be here," Dick said.

"Have a seat, Dick. Good to have you with us again!" Annie said. "I'm brewing up some coffee and we can talk a bit before I start to work on my laundry.

"I'd love a cup of coffee," Dick said, "but I'd like to take you gals out for a bite at your fabulous diner after."

"I know Joanie would love it," Annie said, "but I'm way too behind in my laundry."

"You're laundry, pooh!" Joan whispered to Annie. But she was grateful to be given the time alone. Dick was way to kind to simply invite only Joan, and Annie knew it.

Later as Joan and Dick walked toward the diner, they held hands like high school kids and looked into store windows. The gentle breeze offered the scent of Dick's aftershave to Joan like a romantic airborne greeting card.

Dick spotted a model display in Kresge's window. "Now that's a model airplane," he said. "Look at that detail!"

"What kind is it?" Joan asked.

"That one there in the front is an English plane, the de Havilland. It's a good plane, but heavy and harder to maneuver than those German Fokker Ds back there. They are flown by the Germans, but I think it's Dutch made."

"You know a lot about planes, then?"

"I once thought I might try to pilot. I thought I might have the skill needed. But, well, things change."

"Yes, they do," Joan said nodding.

Arriving at the diner, they took a booth that looked out on the street. Joan felt transformed. She could hardly remember what she had done that morning. Everything seemed so joyful, so alive inside. She didn't want to waste a second of it, not even to take the time to breathe.

"Yes, I'll have two eggs, toast, potatoes, do you have bacon today? Okay, and bacon and orange juice. And a cup of coffee to start with. How about you, honey? Whatever you want."

Joan felt like a queen. "Well, I think I'd like some bacon and baking soda biscuits if you have those, and oh, and coffee, too. Thank you."

Dick was about to ask Joan if she'd like some eggs or home fries, but he was too late. At the words thank you, the waitress was off and running. He smiled. "I forgot about her," he said.

"There's nobody like her!" Joan giggled. "Well, except the other waitress here."

It was true. The waitresses at the Abbottsville Diner were legendary. Aside from their prowess in a pair of rubber soled shoes, they also had spectacular hearing.

"Thank you," said their waitress as she sped by with someone else's breakfast.

Joan giggled again.

Across the aisle and down ten booths, a dark shadow was secretly advancing an agenda, weighing the conditions, the opportunity, and probabilities, and formulating a plan of attack.

Like the agile Fokker, she rose and spun enjoying the sparkle and dazzle of her jewelry, her newly styled hair, and expensive burgundy dyed in the wool suit. She examined the perfect shining burgundy and gold heels for any imperfections they might have picked up along the way. They passed inspection.

A waitress buzzed through, extracting her plate and asking if there would be anything else.

"Yes," said the shadow, "but I'll handle it."

The waitress paused an uncharacteristic three seconds to react, and then she was off again.

Someone put money in the jukebox and Glen Miller's music filled the atmosphere. Back at Joan and Dick's booth, the waitress was clearing away the plates, and it occurred to Joan that she and Dick had spent most of the morning cooing like lovebirds.

I need to ask about our plans, Joan thought. But I don't want to be a nag. She was still thinking when Dick took her hand from across the table. It was electric. She caught her breath again, secretly wondering if it was dangerous to her heart to be doing that all the time.

"You look so nice," he said. "This is such a warm place. I hope we always have it. We could make it a tradition."

Joan smiled. "What a lovely thought. Sunday at the diner!"

They sipped coffee and Dick toyed with the idea of having a slice of apple pie with ice cream.

Then Joan said, "So how is everything with your mom? It must have been so hard to go home, having lost your father."

"She's doing pretty well," Dick said. "She amazes me. I thought she might close in and stop enjoying life, but I think she looks at it as a new phase. It was nice to spend some time with her."

"Were you there the whole time?"

"Pretty much—" It was then that the shadow descended on their table. The overreaching, undercutting, well-dressed shadow of Gloria Marini.

"Dick!" she said, reaching across Joan to hug Dick and kiss him on the cheek. She left red lip prints on his jaw that instantly glared at Joan. "It's so nice to see you! I didn't think you'd be back again so soon!"

"Uh—" began Dick, looking at Gloria, and then at Joan, and back at Gloria.

"You're such a charmer," said Gloria, shoving Joan on the shoulder. "I just wanted to thank you so much for the nice card. I was so surprised to hear from you!"

Joan's mouth fell open. What was she talking about? Gloria had received a card from Dick? When? Why? And where was her own card from Dick? She looked at Dick, instantly wishing that she'd spent fewer minutes cooing and a couple more minutes interrogating.

"Well," said Dick, still taken aback. "You're welcome." He nodded toward Joan, and back to Gloria.

"You look great as usual," said Gloria. She gave him a coquettish look, turned, and said over her shoulder, "I hope this visit is as much fun as your last one!" Then she shook her shiny red curls at Joan and strutted down the aisle to her booth.

Joan felt flattened, her entire morning of floating on air grounded by the thirty-second invasion.

"What did she mean, this visit?" was the first thing she said. "Were you here recently? When I didn't know about it?"

"Not, well no, I just got in yesterday—"

"Yesterday! You were here Saturday night and you didn't call?"

"Oh, no, Joan, I was going to call, but then I thought I'd wait until today to tell you—"

"Wait? Do you know how long I've been waiting to hear something from you? Just a note or a phone call, or even a message from Bob or somebody. But nothing, Dick, nothing, it's been weeks!"

"I know, I'm sorry, but if you—"

"And now I come to find out that this woman, this predatory redhead has not only received a card from you, she's been seeing you as well!"

"Oh, no, that's not—"

"I know she's pretty, and wealthy, and every other good thing that I'm not, but we were supposed to be engaged, Dick. You and me, not you and her!" Joan's voice was rising as the days and weeks of frustration poured out of her. "I thought I was the one, not her!"

"Joan, you are, it's just that—"

"Do you deny that you sent her that card, then?"

"No, I don't deny that, but I only did it—"

"And nothing! Not a thing for me, no card, no call—who am I? The Sunday stand-in while the hot Saturday night date sleeps in and dresses up for the next night out?"

Dick had stopped objecting. The whole lovely morning had suddenly turned sour. He felt powerless to change or even interrupt the tide of emotion that was bearing down on him. It was like a dark wave that he couldn't fight or even see a path clear through.

But still Joan carried on. "Every time she pushed her way in between us, from that very first night, I wondered if one day she would get her hooks into you. If she could use all that money and glamour to lure you away from me. Why did you even bother to stop by to see me this morning if you've got her?"

Somewhere in her mind, Joan was telling herself to stop, to shut up, to listen to Dick, to ease up. But she couldn't do it. And when her tirade came to rest at that final reckless question, she took a look at Dick's face. His expression was new to her. It was almost resigned. So maybe I'm right about all of this, she thought. At that point, she stood and flounced out of the diner.

Dick had not mentioned that he had caught cold, and that he had been put on medication to avoid reconnecting with the awful illness that had nearly done him in the month preceding Christmas. But the color drained from his face as the love he knew appeared to be evaporating before his eyes and he felt a deep sorrow down to his bones. He hadn't known Joan was so upset. He had thought she understood, that she knew he had been thinking of her and dreaming of the moments they would be reunited.

Worst of all, he hadn't been guilty of anything but writing a two-line thank you to Gloria in care of Father Bertrand for her condolence card on the death of his father. She had somehow managed to make it look as though he'd been spending time with her during separate trips and had carried out some great correspondence between the two of them. But there had been nothing. He was innocent.

Chapter Eight

Dick stood at the bus stop, his light overcoat being no match for the increasing wind and drop in temperature. He coughed and reached for his handkerchief. What had just happened, he wondered. One minute, he and Joan had been enjoying the most wonderful meal at the diner, just the two of them locked in a magnificent arena all their own. It had been another world, a completely new and beautiful place for him, full of possibilities. Everything he had seen as they walked along in this fascinating woman's town was different and interesting to him.

He coughed again, harder, and pulled his collar up further. He should have worn the wooly scarf Joan had crocheted for him, he thought. But even that thought cut like a knife through the painfully recent memory. What had happened back there? Had that been the premature end to the bliss he had been chasing his whole adult life?

He heard a train whistle in the distance. It seemed so shrill to be so far away, he thought. His ears began to throb, and he covered one of them with his ungloved hand. It felt warm to the touch. Shortly after, it felt to Dick as though a hot poker connected his two ears and sent fire down his throat.

He took a deep breath to thwart his growing dizziness. The bus stop post was mercifully close by and he was able to lean on it for support. By the time the bus came, he was barely able to get up the steps and inside. He felt around for change, finding he had exactly twenty cents left, remembering that he had accidently forgotten his change from the check on the table, and tipped the waitress separately as well. She must have thought it was her lucky day, he told himself, trying to perk up.

Finding a seat near the front, Dick sat and tried once again to make sense of what had happened with Joan.

Gloria. It had all come down to Gloria. The woman, as filled with good intention as she was, had a knack for ruining things between him and Joan. He was sure that's where the whole problem started.

Gloria was an attractive woman, too, if one took stock of her individual attributes. But the whole package, as Bob liked to say, was somehow not the same, it was not the sum of the parts; it was lesser than the sum of the parts. Math thoughts came to him then; creating equivalents on either side of the equal sign; if one takes 6G from this side, one must also take 6G from the other side.

He shook his head and tried to stay alert. How long
was the bus ride? On the way into town, he had
counted 6 bus stops. How many had they gone? Oh
and what was his address? He would know how to
find it, but which street should he ask for?

"How long you been home, Soldier?" asked an
older gentleman as he swung into the seat across the
aisle.

"Two months, Sir," said Dick.

"Glad you made it back."

"Thank you, Sir."

"Although I don't mind saying, you look a little
worse for the wear."

Dick squinted. Did he just say I look like a little
horse over there? He smiled, hoping that would satisfy
the man.

The man continued to talk, and Dick strained to
listen. But he may as well have relaxed. The older
fellow had no intention of stopping his lengthy diatribe
on the nasty experience that was World War One. It
continued on for about five minutes. And while Dick
on any other day might have listened with sincere
interest, that day his primary objective was to stay
awake.

Finally, the bus came to a stop that Dick recognized
as his own. The apartment he shared with Bob lay only
half a block in from the main road and it was a
benevolently brief walk.

The hallway was warm and smelled of a
combination of Sunday dinners. He exhaled as the hot
pain in his head seemed to fade. Inside his apartment,
he found a note from Bob saying he was having dinner
with Laureen's family.

Dick started to put on some coffee, but remembered the collection of teas his mother had insisted he take with him, and began to heat some hot water. His coughing had returned, and he felt the heat in his throat seeming to fire up his chest. The kettle quickly came to a whistling boil, and as he poured his tea, which was an herbal one that smelled of fresh flowers, he decided it would be a good idea to take his medicine.

But where had he put it? Barely with the strength to manage his teacup over to the little couch in their living/dining room, he decided to wait and have it before he went to bed that night.

So he rested back against the couch, drank the tea, and then drifted into sleep.

On Joan's return home, with the wind rising and the clouds darkening, she continued to stew over the nerve of some people. She wasn't one hundred percent sure which people had dished out the nerve, but she knew she'd been hurt and by golly it was somebody's fault!

Just barely see him myself, but he was already in conversation with her, she thought, kicking a tin can hard toward the gutter.

"I wouldn't do that if I were you," came a cheerful voice behind her. "There's a war on, you know. We're supposed to save all metals and metal products."

Joan looked up to see Bernice. For once, she was not a welcome sight. Joan wanted the luxury of pouting and pounding all by herself without someone else getting involved.

"I was just kidding," Bernice said smiling, as she picked up the can.

"Okay," Joan said.

"Hey, what's wrong, Joan?" Bernice asked.

"Nothing. Everything," Joan said. "Everything in the whole world!"

"Hey, what is it?" Bernice said, taking her elbow to comfort her. "You look really upset."

"That's because I am upset!" Joan said. "I just went to a nice breakfast with Dick—"

"Dick? Is he back in town?"

"No, I imagined it!"

"Sorry, go on."

"And we're just talking and I'm just about to ask him what he's been doing all this time, and along comes his other girlfriend."

"Other girlfriend? What are you talking about?" Bernice said laughing. "There ain't no other girlfriend."

"Well, tell that to Gloria Marini!" Joan said, fairly yelling.

"Shh, Joanie," Bernice said, half laughing, half alarmed. "We're out in public."

Joan shook it off and said, "Well if you want to know, it turns out he's been seeing her, writing to her all this time. That's why I never see him."

"Oh I don't believe that!" Bernice said, trying to comfort her. "We would have seen him around town, surely."

"Well, if you don't believe me, fine," said Joan, and stomped across the street barely watching for traffic.

Bernice watched her go. Joan was never rude. What in the world had happened? What she'd said about Gloria and Dick, that just could not be true. But if it weren't, why did she think it? She shook her head watching Joan make her way down the walk. It was impossible to remember a time when she'd seen Joan that way. Something must have really set her off.

The previous night had been such fun, all of them together missing the St. Valentine's Day dance, enjoying each other's company, relieved not to be alone. No one had received any flowers, at least to her knowledge, and there were no broken hearts, just fun, laughter, and of course the end phases of their colds.

Maybe that was the problem! Maybe Joan's cold had come back with a vengeance and she was not herself. It could be, Bernice decided, but she didn't seem to be sick. She just seemed mad.

Bernice retraced her steps, deciding to stop in and pay a visit at St. Benedict's. After all, she had planned to before she saw Joan, and on Sunday evenings, the church was so quiet and beautiful.

Opening the heavy wooden door, she was surprised to find it so warm inside. She stood looking straight ahead for a few moments, just taking in the beauty of the surroundings. The peace she had always sought there would never fail to embrace her.

She fished through her pockets for change, made her offering and lit a candle. She knelt in front of the beautiful statue of the Madonna. The eyes of the figure seemed almost to be looking right at Bernice. They were kind and gentle, and gave Bernice the feeling she was being hugged warmly.

She relaxed against the kneeler and looked up at the Madonna like a little child looking at her mother. A kind of peace came over her, one which she had experienced many times before, but one that she sorely needed that afternoon.

Grabbing her purse, she moved to a pew nearby and leaned back, gazing up at the crucifix. So many things had changed over the last year. Her decision to enter the Convent, their requirement that she wait, her inheritance, the loss of much of her inheritance to overdue taxes, the grocery store purchase, the plans in the works for the school—and Henry.

How she loved Henry. But now with him gone, so much of the fun of life was also gone. She wanted to cry. Her love wasn't romantic in nature, it was more of an open, sisterly, embracing love. They had dated before, when they were kids just out of high school. But since then, the relationship had grown to be more like family.

Following her decision to devote her life in service to God with the Benedictines, Henry had felt that he, too, had been called. He had decided to see if that indeed were to happen, and left to start his studies only a few weeks before.

With Henry's departure being coincident with Harry's arrival, meaning Helen would be a lot less free, Bernice's two closest friends were no longer very available.

She closed her eyes and prayed first for the problems that her friends were all going through to get quickly resolved. Don't let them continue to suffer even after the men have come back home, she prayed. She paused and looked into the eyes of the Madonna. And the tears began to come.

"I'm so lonely, Blessed Mother," she whispered. "I'm so very, very lonely."

As she cried, it was as if she were breaking free from a prison. Her heart began to feel lighter, and her mood lifted. I hope there's no one in here besides me, she thought. They might send me to the cry room. She thought of Mrs. St. John holding her in her lap as a grown woman and it made her giggle. What is wrong with me? I'm praying and making jokes at the same time.

What next? Pirouettes on a tight rope? Having lost the thread of the conversation, Bernice decided it was time to go. But as she turned to go, looking up she noticed the old choir loft. For one mortifying second, she feared that Bitsy, the choir director, was sitting up there listening to her while pretending to look over her music. But to her relief, she found she was alone.

Somehow though, she felt moved by the sight of that elevated loft, remembering its back stairways that creaked and smelt of waterlogged basements. It had been over a year since she had traveled those steps. So much had happened since then. Yet, in some ways, especially standing there in the silent church, it felt much more recent. Her love of music had not died or even faltered. It was alive and well. In fact, she had ordered a radio to set up in her grocery store so that shoppers could enjoy the shows and music as they shopped. It was a revolutionary investment, she was told. But she had never minded being somewhat original, as she preferred to think of herself. And the idea seemed likely to catch on.

But that afternoon inside the embracing walls of St. Benedict's Church, inhaling the rich scent of incense and the candles, seeing their tiny but living flames through the rich blue translucent votive holders, Bernice experienced an epiphany.

"I've been missing this!" she said softly. She turned to look at the face of the Madonna. "It's music, isn't it?" she said, wide-eyed. "This music."

She grabbed her things and went to the back of the church, and bounded up the old staircase, opened the door to the loft and took a deep breath.

Everything was as she'd last seen it. The organ was in the same place, masses of music, disorganized and spilling over the edges. The choir member's chairs were still arranged willy nilly, although there were markedly fewer of them and they looked a little worn out.

Standing at the doorway, she could almost see Bitsy, the neurotic choir director, frantically searching through music, trying to find something she had mislaid, and then turning to blame some unfortunate tenor or alto. Bernice giggled at the thought, always glad to be seated as soprano at a safer distance.

She looked at the chair that had once been occupied by Ella, now deceased, probably singing with the Choir of Angels in Heaven, she thought. And Nan and Jack, too. Magnificent vocalist gone to God.

Would it make sense to come back to that choir, she wondered, with its odd director who had seemed unpredictable and often times more irascible and injurious than a rattlesnake? Bernice was tough on the outside, and she could accept or deflect rudeness or poorly delivered criticism, but it wasn't quite as easy for her to watch the less resilient members of the choir being maltreated. She knew that at this point in her life, she would not sit still for it. Still, to be in a choir, she thought, it was a precious gift. It wasn't only the singing but being in the midst of such heavenly sound.

The conflict within her wasn't giving way. Her love for the music was overwhelming her. She knew now that she had missed the music like an old friend no less than she was missing Henry and her time with Helen. But was this particular choir something she needed to return to?

She looked at the old familiar, beautiful but painful choir loft, sadly shook her head and backed away.

Chapter Nine

"Joanie's a good singer," Annie said to Bernice as they put away the dishes that night.

"Joan," Bernice said nodding. "How is she feeling?"

"Awful."

"That was the feeling I got."

"Why, what do you mean?"

"The other day when I saw her in the street. She like to take my head off!"

"You're kidding. Joanie?"

"Yeah."

"What was it all about?" Annie said, putting down the dishtowel and sitting down. "Were you joking with her or something?"

"No, to tell you the truth, all I did was try to help her see the bright side."

"Bright side?"

"Yeah, she said that Dick was supposedly seeing Gloria Marini—"

"Oh that, yeah."

"Don't tell me you believe it?"

"No, that's ridiculous. I don't even think she believes it anymore. She just jumped at the first possible explanation about where he'd been for so long."

"Didn't she just ask him?"

"No, you know, that's our problem. We're so used to getting no information that we don't expect it. We just accept it—up to a point. Then we want to know the rest of the story. And when Gloria showed up at that diner and filled in the blanks, Joan was ready for a fight."

"It shoulda been with Gloria."

"No," said Joan, forlornly entering the kitchen. "It should have been with me. I'm the all-time biggest idiot. Hi Bernice."

"Hey Joan. I didn't mean nothin'—"

"Don't worry about it. You were right. And I'm sorry I was so rude to you on the street there. I know you were only trying to shed a better light on what had happened."

"Let's sit in the living room," said Annie. "This chair is hard as a brick."

"Good idea," said Joan. Taking comfort in the fluffy chair beside the sofa, she sighed. "I guess no one's getting married in this house."

"Not you guys, too! Did you and Sly have a blowup?" Bernice said to Annie.

"No, no, she was just talking about how long it's taking."

"Right and how expensive, don't forget that, too," Joan added. "Hey, this is a nice chair."

"You don't really think it's over between you and Dick, do you?" Bernice asked. "That's impossible!"

"Everything's possible," Joan said glumly. "I'm sure he's gone back home wondering what he ever bothered to come up here for."

Bernice started to speak but Annie shook her head. "Let her wallow," she said as they returned to the kitchen. "She needs it."

"Whatever you say," said Bernice. "I was just going to ask her if she wanted to join my choir."

"Oh!" Annie laughed. "Sorry! Ask her, great idea."

"Yo Joanie," Bernice called. "You still in there?"

"Barely."

"Can you roust yourself enough to sit in the kitchen? We won't put you to work."

"All right." She padded slowly into the kitchen, her head down and hands in her robe pocket. "I should be doing those dishes."

"Hey listen," said Bernice, ignoring her comment, "I'm thinking of starting a small choir group. Just for pretty hymns and sacred music. Do you want to join?"

"Are you sure you want me?"

"Yes."

"You haven't heard me sing."

"Annie says you're good."

"Thanks, Annie. I don't know Bern, I feel so sick right now, I don't know if I want to do anything."

"Well, if you don't want to do anything right now, that's fine, because I'm just kind of putting it together. I only need about eight to ten people," Bernice said patiently, but making a face at Annie.

Annie turned away to hide her reaction.

"You are," Bernice said, "the bright star here. You are pretty, talented, and the nicest person I know."

"Hey!" said Annie.

"On the nicest team of people I know is what I meant to say," corrected Bernice.

Annie giggled and even Joan gave it a smile. "It does sound kind of nice," she said. "Can we do Panis Angelicus?"

"Yes!" said Bernice. "Absolutely!"

"Well okay, then. I want to do it. But you'll have to hear me first."

"No I don't. Good, that makes two of us. Annie?"

"I'll do it. I'm good."

"Yeah, you're good. Modest, too. Okay, that makes three."

Annie wrung out the dishtowel, which was wet from drying the dishes so soon after they were washed, and hung it on the oven door. "Let's have a little bite and we can talk over what kind of songs to do."

"Great," said Bernice. "Joan, could you take notes? Your handwriting is the best."

"Sure."

As Joan went to the desk in the living room to get a pencil and some paper, someone knocked on the door.

"Laureen!" Joan cried when she opened the door. "Come on in!"

"Hello Laureen!" said Annie. "How are you doing these days?"

"Great!" she said. "I'm just here for a second. Bob is in the car. I just wanted to—oh, Bernice, you're here, too!"

Laureen paused and dashed across the room to give Bernice a hug. "You are such a lifesaver!" she said smiling.

Bernice smiled.

"Okay, I'm confused. What did she do?" Annie asked.

"Nothing," said Bernice.

"Yeah, nothing," said Laureen, "except help me and Bob set the date! She's given Bob the job of store manager at the grocery store! We'll be able to afford to save for a wedding and have a little house and everything! Before you know it, we'll all be married and having our families just like we dreamed!" She was so filled with cheer and happiness, she never noticed that there was a mild shadow across the room. Her eyes gleamed with the deep joy she felt and her golden hair had luster and life as it swung around with her as she moved.

Joan, for all the bittersweet she felt, could not help but be moved by the innocence and beauty of Laureen's happiness. Her childhood friend had always been a source of support and inspiration. Now as she saw the love in her eyes, she was grateful for Laureen's happiness and genuinely wished her the world they'd always dreamed of as youngsters.

"And I want you all to be bridesmaids," Laureen was saying, "and the gowns will be beautiful, you'll see! Oh we have so much to do—the invitations need to be sent out six weeks ahead you know, and we can't send them out until we know where and when. So it's full speed ahead!" she finished, making a comical gesture.

"Oh Laureen what great news!" said Bernice.

"Yes, and congratulations! It will be a wonderful celebration!" said Annie.

"We'll be happy to help out, and of course we'll all be bridesmaids, too," said Joan.

Laureen took a few steps toward Joan. "Oh no, not you, Joan," she said, startling everyone. "I want you to be my Maid of Honor."

Joan hugged her friend, tears of both happiness and sorrow gathering in her eyes. "Thank you, Laureen," she said, "I'm honored that you've asked me."

After a short visit, Laureen left, eager to get back to Bob and make plans.

"That's one down and two to go," said Bernice as she closed the door behind Laureen.

"Don't forget Margaret," said Joan. "Three to go."

"It's going to be wedding central around here," said Annie.

"Maybe," said Joan.

"Definitely," said Annie firmly. "We're going to sort everything out."

"Yep," said Bernice. "Now, if we could get back to where we were?"

"Are you going to work tomorrow, Joanie?" Annie asked.

"I had better or they'll fire me," said Joan. "I don't want to risk losing this job. You never know."

"Well, that's true. You never know."

"Yeah," said Bernice, "Dick is gonna make her his work slave, while he stays at home drinking beer and playing cards."

The absurdity of her remark made even Joan laugh.

"All right, all right," said Joan. "I will try to stay positive about this. But I still need his address so I know where to write!"

"Right now, write down these songs," Bernice said, looking at Annie.

"Oh me? I get to choose? Great. I say, first Joan's song, Panis Angelicus. And I want Ave Verum Corpus, and of course Ave Maria."

"Which one?" said Joan.

"Both!" said Annie. "And How Great Thou Art."

"Hold on, hold on, I'm not a machine," said Joan.

"I'd like to do the Hallelujah from the Messiah," said Bernice.

"Oh we can't possibly do that with only 8 people!" said Annie.

"Well, we could adapt it. We could maybe smooth out some of the parts, and blend the men's voices together."

"Gosh, men," said Annie. "Who do we know that sings?"

"Bob sings," said Joan. "Laureen says he's great, and I've heard him sing a little myself."

"Can he hold a tune?"

"Well, he sang White Christmas to her last Christmas. It was really romantic."

"That's not the same kind of music," Bernice said. "It's easier."

"Yeah," said Joan. "We could give him an audition."

Everybody laughed. "Laureen would love that!" said Bernice. "No, I'll ask him next time we get together about the store. That's going to be one busy man, though; store, wedding, and maybe choir?"

"No, the wedding will be mostly in Laureen's court," said Joan. "He's going to be gung-ho about the great job you gave him. That's where his enthusiasm is going, I'm sure."

The girls talked until late, and since it was after ten o'clock, invited Bernice to stay over, which she gladly accepted.

"It's too bad we don't have a third bedroom," said Annie. "You might as well live here."

"Yeah," said Joan. "Now that Helen's got a man over there." The girls giggled.

"I do miss her," said Annie.

"Me, too," said Bernice. "If you want to know the truth of it, until tonight, I was miserable.

Joan put an arm around her. "What do you mean?" she asked. "Did I do that? I'm so sorry Bernice. I really was a stinker."

"No, well, that probably added to it, to be honest, but I was missing everybody. I was missing Henry the most, no offense."

"Oh?" said Annie.

"No, not like that," Bernice said shaking her head. "He was my kind of charge at first, then he was my friend, and we went everywhere together. But after Christmas I got busy trying to find a school and take care of the store, and he was working on finding a monastery, which I did not realize. So it was pretty sudden and sad when he left."

"Gosh," said Joan. "I had no idea."

"No, because you were with Dick until a few weeks ago, and Annie had Sly and all, you know. And I used to have Helen, too, but as you can imagine she's a little tied up right now."

"Well, that won't last," said Annie.

"Oh my gosh, don't tell me Harry's going back in—not again!" Joan said.

"No, I mean it's new and fun now, but you know Harry. He's not going to sit around the house for long. He'll be out looking for something before you know it."

"Yeah, said Joan. If he's not already!"

"I don't want Helen to be lonely," Bernice said. "I just want to see her again myself."

"She probably feels exactly the same way," said Annie. "Let me get you some blankets. How many pillows do you like?"

"Two."

"Okay Joan, give her yours."

Joan laughed. "I'll give her yours," she said. "I think I broke mine."

"Well I accidentally lit mine on fire, and they're all burnt up."

"Well, after I broke them, I also spilled vegetable oil on mine.

"And once mine got burnt up, I found a bees nest in there."

"I'll stick with the couch pillows," Bernice said scowling. "I didn't realize you guys were so possessive about your pillows!"

"Well you can still have mine if you like," Joan offered giggling.

After all the frivolity, and lights were finally out, Bernice gazed out the window, and seeing the moon through the clouds, gave a prayer of thanks. "I'm never alone with You," she whispered. "Thank you."

Several miles away on the road home from Atlantic City to Abbottsville, Gloria sat in a taxicab, thinking about her date and evaluating how it had gone.

He put me in a cab, she thought. Does that mean I'm special, that he wants a professional to drive me rather than take a chance himself? Or does it mean he'd like to get rid of me as quickly as he could? Oh that's not possible, of course. She snickered.

She had certainly shown him her good taste. She had ordered a steak, and when hers was brought out, and it turned out to be very thin and overdone, she made no bones about rejecting it. Surely that impressed him, she thought.

And what about the wines? Nobody knew expensive wine like she did. She was sure it was admiration she had seen in her wide-eyed date when she ordered the fifteen-year-old French claret. Their departure hadn't been particularly romantic, though, and she wondered about the man's odd behavior when he got the check, and mysterious conversations with the kitchen manager, but never mind. He was definitely impressed with her.

As the cab approached her street, she caught sight of a man taking a stroll in the dark. There's a brave one, she thought. I wonder if he'll run into trouble with the Civil Defense. Maybe he is Civil Defense.

"Driver," she said, "Slow down as we pass this man."

The driver was a cooperative type, although he gave her a knowing look, as if to say, I get you, you like to have a collection of men on the string.

His look was lost on her, however, as she strained through the dark to see if the man was who she thought he might be. He had that same hard to define manner about him, a walk that said I'm in control, but I'm not a bad guy. She found it irresistible.

After the vehicle had driven alongside him, slowing down to give her enough time to give him the once over, Gloria sat back in the cab, relaxed, a smile on her face and a plan on her mind. Never had she been so happy to see someone. It was time to finally put that Joan Foster in her place!

The next morning, Bob McGarrett shaved and showered, and imagined he was shaving and showering in the house that he and his wonderful Laureen would soon share. She was a catch and he knew it. When he was ready to leave, he stopped and tapped on Dick's door.

"You never shoulda gone out last night," he said as Dick opened it, looking disheveled. "You're not coming in today."

"I'd like to make a few hours anyway," Dick said, although he was obviously not well.

"Look, there's no rush at this point. I'm still getting things straightened out with the previous manager. Once that's done, I'll really need you. Besides, when my wedding comes up, I'll want someone strong and well to be Assistant Manager and take over when I'm off. So the last thing I want is for you to let this thing really take hold and put you back in sick bay. Or you know, the hospital."

Dick was disappointed. He knew that what Bob was saying made sense. Why had he gone out the night before anyway, he wondered. Walking on a cold night was probably one of the worst things a person fighting illness could do. But he knew Bob would be fair with him. "Will you let me make up the hours next week?"

"I'll insist on it. You're good until then, Buddy. Your money is completely worthless until you get your first paycheck. And I'll know when that is."

Dick smiled, reaching for a handshake. "Thanks, Buddy."

"Yep. I got your back. My turn now." He smiled.

After Bob had left to meet up with Bernice, Dick took the medicine he had been prescribed, shaved, got a hot shower, and wrapped up in a warm robe and pajamas and enjoyed the coffee that Bob had left, keeping warm on the little stove.

It was a comfortable place, and he was secure. Bob was the best friend any man could have. He knew that. But he was still miserable. He hadn't told Bob about the fight with Joan because it still barely seemed real to him.

But as the days wore on, and neither of them contacted the other, he wondered if the thing really was over.

Then a frightening thought came to mind. What if that Gloria character believed what Joan believed; that he and she were dating? She was a pretty girl and seemed to have a knack for showing up wherever he went, outside of the war in Europe. The mental image of that made him smile. The idea of seeing her paddling up the river, or riding a mule up the side of a mountain wearing her fancy jewelry, clothing, and shoes, all made up and styled was ridiculous. She would get off the mule, he thought, land perfectly, and say, "Hi Dick! I just thought I'd drop in to say hello."

He chuckled out loud. She was a character. Nevertheless, she wasn't for him. He'd never even considered her. Once he'd met Joan, just barely seen her on the steps of the Chalfont Hotel, there had been no one else. But maybe it had not been the same for her. It was hard to tell with some women what they were thinking.

And too, if she were sorry for her tirade at the diner, realized that he hadn't been running around behind her back, why didn't she come and tell him that? Apologize for her accusations that she'd made without giving him a chance to defend himself.

Women were hard to figure.

It did not occur to Dick that while he knew he was living there with Bob, Joan, only a bus ride away, did not. Rather than talk about practical matters during their brief reunion, they had opted to stare at each other and read each other's thoughts of love and devotion. So while hoping to defeat the recurrence of his illness, Dick waited to hear from Joan, without any chance of her contacting him, or even knowing where he was.

Chapter Ten

Annie was in the shop bright and early that morning, happy to be doing something and ready to work on some new displays. The vesper shop was quickly becoming a very special place to her. While before, it had been a way to earn some money, now, it was still that but also a place to indulge her creative urges. With so many beautiful things to work with, she never tired of arranging and rearranging them.

She reached for one of the angels, narrowly missing knocking one off the shelf. Her heart skipped as she caught it and pushed it in, further from the edge. Its reflection was large and arcing in morning sun as it streamed richly through the window.

She paused to study the other statues there and inside the cases. Seeing the small resin statue of Our Lady of Grace amongst many other statues of the Blessed Mother, she gave way to the memory of that tall, dark, and impossibly attractive man that had come through her door in search of Our Lady of Grace. He'd been referred to her shop by someone in town and was urgently seeking whatever was available to take home as a gift. She remembered showing him the beautiful statue she had, with silvery robes and roses all the way down her gown. He had bought it, not even thinking about the price.

At the time, she thought what a lucky girlfriend he has. But it had turned out to have been a gift for his mother, and Annie shortly thereafter actually became the lucky girlfriend. She had been hopelessly smitten ever since.

His time in the service had tempered Sylvester a little, and he was more careful with money, but he was still that loving, handsome, smart, and gentle man, a fact which she thanked God for every day. She thought of the mental agonies that some of the men had suffered and she wondered sometimes how Sly had escaped those terrible problems, especially considering some of the experiences he had had.

Grateful that he and his buddies, all the men really, and women too, over there, were willing to go through all of it to keep everyone at home protected, she closed her eyes and thanked God again. It had been so hard, all of those months, hearing nothing, knowing nothing, fearing everything. Until that wonderful, overwhelmingly beautiful Christmas night only months before. It was still fresh on her mind, his dramatic entrance, their hilarious collision, and the days that followed.

She relived bits and pieces of the dream as she dusted the statues of the small children that were part of a little crowd who sat listening to Jesus. They were so beautifully painted and so delicately shaped.

"We'll have some children like this," she thought happily out loud. "It won't be long now, since he's back home."

Smiling she looked around for the right colors of construction paper to begin putting together her scenery and backdrop.

A few blocks away, Bob eased his old car into a spot behind Bernice's grocery store. The rear walls of the building were starting to crumble, and the base, although brick, seemed uneven, as if it were settling. One of the windows in the service door was cracked and the loading dock looked rickety and unstable.

This might be more of a job than I thought, Bob said to himself. As he got out of his car, he noticed an old car sitting in the back lot there had only three wheels. On the fourth side, two cinder blocks supported it.

He knocked on the back door. Immediately it was opened by an older gentleman wearing a leather vest over his rolled up shirt sleeves, dusty black trousers and a visor. For a split second, Bob thought he was in the back room of a newspaper office.

"Hello," he said smiling, "I'm Bob McGarrett."

"Oh come on in, young fellow," said the man. "The little gal said you'd be coming around today. She's just getting settled."

Bob found Bernice in a makeshift office, moving things to make room for her purse. When Bob saw her, his heart sank. The desk was covered with various sizes and colors of papers, bunches of pages stapled together, magazines, and some coffee cups and cartons of some sort. The walls had lists, calendars, schedules, and even some paintings tacked up, while on the floor surrounding the desk were stacks and stacks of papers. They looked like old records or possibly ledger pages.

"Hello Bernice," Bob said forcing a smile. "How are you doing?"

"Take a look around, you can see how I'm doing!" she answered cheerfully. "Pull up that chair and we can talk. Oh, this is Mr. Freiden. Mr. Freiden, this is Bob McGarrett."

"Thanks," said Mr. Freiden. "We've met. I'll get out of your hair. Make sure there's no one out there robbing me." He smiled as he headed for the front of the store.

"Thanks for coming in," Bernice said. "I don't think Mr. Freiden's going to be with us much longer."

"Oh?"

"I mean he's planning to head for Canada as soon as he gets his freedom. I told him you probably wouldn't need more than a few days with him here."

Bob blinked unintentionally. "A few days?" Bob exclaimed before he could control his shock.

"More?" said Bernice.

"Well," Bob began, "from the looks of the office here, I will need to shift it into high gear. Things look a little disheveled. Sorry to be so blunt."

"That's okay," said Bernice, shaking her head. "I know it's bad. Freiden is more of a salesman than a recordkeeper. I don't know much about business, to be honest, but I have already spotted some oversights.

As the two of them worked through the morning, Bob found that while Bernice claimed not to know much about business, she was very sharp and had already gone a long way toward making sense of the mess that Freiden would leave behind.

"I think you've done incredibly well in a very short period of time, Bernice," he said, as he gathered the payables he could find within the collection. "You seem to know how to organize, even if you don't know specifically how it's helping."

"Thanks, Bob!" Bernice said. "I think those words will go a long way toward boosting my self-confidence. It's been needing some mending lately."

"I'm glad it helps, but my words are truthful. You're good at this. If you've got other fish to fry, that's understandable, but I just wanted you to know that you've made it possible for me to meet that 'few days' deadline that scared me a few hours ago."

"How about some lunch?" Bernice asked. "One of the fringe benefits will be to have your pick of the fresh fruit, cheeses or bakery breads. I'm even thinking it would be a good idea to bring in a coffee percolator and hot plate."

"That's great," said Bob. "Although I'd hold off on the hot plate until we get a safe, paper-free spot for it!" They laughed.

Later as they finished up their lunch, and gathered up the linens that Bernice had laid out on part of the desk, Bernice said casually, "I hear you do a little singing."

Bob chuckled. "I do like to sing," he said. "But it's been a while. How about you?"

"Oh I love it! And what you said about me doing organizing stuff—well, I do kind of have a knack for it sometimes. I like to put together projects. And one of them I've come up with recently is to start a sort of a choir. I'm putting together maybe 8 or 10 folks to sing sacred hymns, classical pieces, things like that. Joan and Annie said you were excellent."

"Me? Oh, I don't know, Bernice. I'm not really very professional.

"None of us is professional," Bernice said laughing. "Believe me! It's going to be for us and maybe for veterans in the hospitals—"

"Okay, I'm in," Bob said abruptly. "I hadn't thought of whom it would benefit—I'm in for that, and thanks for thinking of it. What an excellent idea."

Bernice smiled. This day was turning out to be very good indeed!

That afternoon as Joan got onto the 2:15 to Abbottsville, she was extremely mindful of sitting near the front of the bus. Once she was seated, she perched on the outside of the seat, not wanting to get caught on the inside again.

Remembering the early morning ride, she shivered. It was surely just a one-time thing, she told herself. But at that point, it was hard to believe it.

She had walked to the bus stop as she normally did, it being quite early in the morning and somewhat dark still. And while that sometimes made her uneasy, it was fine that day and there were no problems. It was when she got on the bus that she encountered the man.

Because a woman with several children had situated them in the first three rows of seats and the next few were occupied, she ended up in a seat not far from the back of the bus. As she had sat there, counting the things on her fingers that she needed to complete that day at work and making a list, a man got on the bus and decided to sit himself down next to her.

She hadn't really noticed him until she got the feeling someone was staring at her. She looked up from her work and was startled to see a very pointy-nosed fellow wearing his hat still staring at her without any shame at all. She looked back down at her list, not knowing what to do.

But the man wasn't satisfied with simply staring at her. He moved his face closer to her, and she could smell some sort of unfamiliar cologne or shaving lotion odor that seemed awfully intense. To rid herself of the smell, she turned toward the window and blocked his view of her work.

She thought her behavior would discourage him, but it seemed only to embolden him. "You're a pretty ting," he said in a very heavily foreign accent. "Why don't you talk wit me?"

"I don't talk to strange men," she said, and I mean strange, she thought.

"I'll buy you a copy," he said, continuing to stare and move in.

"She don't want a copy of nothin', leave her alone," said a short, muscular man sitting behind them. "I been watchin' you, buddy. You just better mind your manners. Lots of room in jail for troublemakers like you."

The strange man immediately withdrew his attentions and sat rigid in his seat, staring straight ahead.

Joan gave the intervening man a look of gratitude, took a deep breath, and went back to her work, although concentrating on anything else was out of the question. If it hadn't been for that tough guy keeping an eye on him, what would that bizarre person have done, she wondered. What copy was he talking about anyway? And what if he was coming on the bus this afternoon?

She sat right in the front all the way home, and grateful for the increasing light in the evenings as February advanced, walked home with no incidents. But the event had rattled her. She thought she had detected a German accent in the man's voice. Another time among many, she regretted her poor behavior toward Dick, and longed for his strong protective arms around her. Maybe, she thought as she neared the house, I will have a letter today!

As Bob drove home that evening, he marveled at this friend of Laureen who was so funny and almost cocky on the outside, but had such a heart of gold on the inside.

After they had spent another hour straightening out the mix of receivables from invoices, gathering what was owed, and totaling what the grocery owed, they set it aside to do the grand totaling the next day. That was Bob's idea.

"It's better to spend a little bit of time away from things before you create the final picture," he said. "When you approach it fresh, you don't have any of the ideas you had in your head while you were gathering the information.

He had thought that would be it for the day, but then Bernice took him to the front of the store to show him yet another set of papers. That set had been more organized and were much easier to understand. As he looked through, noticed the long list of names and addresses, and then the records that corresponded, he began to get the idea.

"These are people you deliver to," he said smiling. "You're giving them a hand."

"Right," Bernice said, "but the names have to stay secret, because people don't want to wear their financial troubles on their sleeves. Many of these families have husbands and providers in the service. But some are actually families of injured or deceased veterans. We want them all protected."

Of course those words had warmed his heart, and at that point, he had become not only fortunate to be the manager of Bernice's grocery, but also proud in a very real way. He didn't think he could describe the gratitude he felt for her kind acts, but she knew. He just smiled, and she nodded, and they went on to other things, including Bernice's little candy bin, filled with penny candies that he was free to offer to the children who came in.

"Dick's going to love this place!" he said as he turned into the apartment's drive. "We're going to have a blast!"

Just then Dick stepped outside, still wearing his robe and pajamas, to pick up the mail.

"I'll get that," Bob said, closing the car door. "You go back inside."

"Fresh air's good for a man," Dick said holding the door open for Bob. "Got any checks in that bundle?"

Bob smiled. "No, probably a bill though. Oh, and here's one for you."

Bob handed him a small, square-shaped envelope with a light pink hue to it. For a few seconds Dick was ecstatic, thinking he had finally heard from Joan. But on closer examination, he could see that it wasn't from

Joan, or from his mother. He was startled but somewhat intrigued to see that it was from Gloria.

"Let me read this in the light," he said to Bob.

"Oh sure," Bob said, who was busy scanning the items on a stationer's bill. "It's probably best on the lamp in the bedroom there."

Dick felt uncomfortable reading the note in front of Bob, not only because he wasn't interested in Gloria, but also because he knew if Bob were aware of his getting the note, the information might end up getting passed to Laureen, and then Joan.

Receiving the letter was not his doing, or his fault, but if a correspondence ensued, that was something different altogether. He was not in favor of something like that.

He opened the note and read in Gloria's very strong penmanship, Dearest Dick, It was such a pleasure to see you in the diner, looking so well and strong. I can't remember when I've been so happy to see someone back home. I'm writing for a very specific reason, though. My father has a very profitable business and is making a point of hiring fellows who have come home from the War. He's very short on managers and thinks that you would be a perfect fit for what he needs. Would you be interested in coming over for coffee to discuss it with him this week? He is looking to make a decision by week's end, so if you please, respond as soon as you can!

Dick put the letter down. How in creation, he wondered, could such a perfect opportunity fall into his lap at such a perfect time? But then he thought about the bigger picture. Why does it have to be Gloria's father? Well, at least it's not Gloria herself. I'm sure she doesn't work there. I wouldn't be spending time with her, only with her father. And maybe not even him. If it's his company, he may not even be there very much. Yes, sir, this could be the perfect opportunity. I think I'll write her back a quick note and let her know I'm up for it.

Then he thought of Bob. I'd better run it by him, Dick thought. He didn't want to be disloyal and he certainly felt Bob had a right to know, considering if he took a job with Gloria's father, he would no longer be able to work for Bob.

He set the letter down on his night table, splashed some water on his face, and went into the kitchen to join Bob rustling up some dinner.

Chapter Eleven

Bob was already throwing some chicken into the oven. "It's probably going to be a little tough," he said to Dick. "They said it might be more of a stewing chicken, considering its age, but roasting should be fine."

"Any way it comes sounds good to me," Dick said. "So how did it go with Bernice today?"

"I gotta tell you, buddy, when I first got there I was wondering if I was going to be able to do the job. That building looks like it's about to fall apart!"

"No kidding," said Dick. "It's brick, isn't it?"

"Yeah, good old brick, but whatever they used to hold it together is not doing the job. She's going to need some brick and block guys," he paused and looked at Dick, "or you!" he laughed. "And then when I got inside, I saw papers and piles of receipts as long as your arm stacked everywhere. It looked like an old hermit had been sleeping there.

Dick laughed. "That must have been pretty bad!"

"But it turned out to be all right. That Bernice, she's got some real genuine qualities, I'll tell you that."

Dick poured himself a glass of milk. "I thought you had yourself a gal," he teased.

"She's got a whole system," Bob continued, ignoring Dick's joke. "She's feeding folks without enough to eat, did you know that?"

"I think I heard something about it, yes, over the holidays."

"Well I didn't. And she has a designated little candy bin she uses as penny candy for the little ones, especially those who don't have the funds. I didn't get to see it in action, but I'm sure that's goodwill all around, from the youngsters on up!"

"Yeah, goodwill, for sure. Did you take management classes in your degree?"

"Yes, I did. They were about the toughest I had to do, but they've stuck with me.

"Goodwill is powerful all right. Not that she needs it. Everybody loves Bernice."

"Well, I guess she deserves it. These days, it's food and survival, and she's right in there, helping out. Kinda makes me wonder if Laureen's and my plans are kind of too much."

"What do you mean, too much?"

"Well, you know, her parents have been saving a long time for her wedding. They have a certain level of quality in mind, including fancy food, fancy place, and fancy dress. With all of this suffering going on, so many people doing with so little, it might be too much, kind of in bad taste, I guess."

"Well if it's fancy though," Dick said, "it could be just what everybody needs. How many guests will there be?"

"I think their list is about 120 people."

Dick whistled. "Boy, that's big!"

"Don't Joan want a big wedding?" Bob said.

His question caught Dick off guard. "Oh," he said pausing, "I, hmm, well, I don't know."

"Hard to believe she's not talking a blue streak about it! These ladies, they've got it all planned out, the color of everything, the flowers."

Dick chuckled stiffly, not sure what to say, not wanting to go into the story about Gloria and the diner. "Gee, I guess you're right."

"You better find out soon," Bob said smiling. "You'll have to start planning a honeymoon to get you out of there!"

"Have you got that taken care of yet?"

"No. No idea what we'll do. But this job is taking me closer, I'll tell you that. And it's going to be bringing you into the fold too, buddy. By the way, what do you think about joining her choir?"

"Over the church?"

"No, Bernice wants to have a sort of independent choir. It'll have maybe some holiday performances, sing for special events, and veterans in hospitals—"

"Count me in," said Dick.

"I had a feeling," Bob said. "What are you, tenor?"

"Oh no, not me. I'm baritone. What are you?"

"I'm baritone, too, I think. So she's gotta get herself some tenors. Keep your ears open for some."

"Listen, Bob," Dick began, "I wanted to talk to you about something. "Even though I'm not sure what I want to do with myself, career wise, I'd like to work at a good job for a little while."

"Hey, no problem!" Bob said, pushing him on the shoulder. "You're hired!"

"And I can't wait to start," Dick said. "But I got this in the mail today." He took Gloria's letter from his pocket.

"That from Joan?"

"No, it's from a gal named Gloria—"

"Gloria? Gloria!"

"You know Gloria Marini?

"No, and from what I hear, I don't want to. I've seen her plenty though. You're not seeing her, too!"

"No, no, no. Nothing like that. She's got some good qualities, but Joan's the only woman for me."

"Well that's good to hear."

"Yeah, listen, she invites me, or rather her father has invited me through her, to come to their place to discuss a management position at his company. I probably wouldn't take it, but I think it would be more money—"

"Are you crazy, man?" Bob interrupted. "Go to work for the father of that woman?"

"Well, I don't think I would see Gloria—"

"It doesn't matter. Man, if you took that job, Joan would hit the roof."

"I know it sounds bad, and it gave me a start, but think about the money. We'd be able to get married much sooner—"

"If you ever got married," Bob said. "No, no, it's a bad idea, buddy. I wouldn't chance it."

Dick was surprised at the intensity of his friend's objections. Maybe I don't know women very well, he thought. He almost broke down and told Bob about the blowup at the diner with Joan, but based on Bob's response in the present conversation, Dick wasn't keen on getting Bob's input on that. Probably he was right not to take the job. It might possibly create more problems than it would solve. But boy the money would be nice. Even though they hadn't talked figures, manager fulltime sounded meatier than Assistant Manager part time.

It couldn't hurt to just go to the meeting, he thought. None of the girls would be there, Bob wouldn't know about it until after it was over. If the offer was really good, he could talk to Joan about it—if he ever talked to Joan again.

Weary from the illness and then all the commotion about the new situation cropping up, he decided to put it out of his mind and enjoy that excellent dinner Bob was cooking up.

However, bright and early the next day, Gloria would receive Dick's handwritten note accepting the offer of conversation, requesting the where and when.

Another invitation went out that day. That one was from Helen, asking Bernice to join her for lunch. I'm so sorry it's been so long, and I probably miss you more than you miss me with all of your activities, but come on over for lunch today if you could, she wrote. I've got some leftover roast to make sandwiches with and after lunch, we can shoo Harry out the door and gab.

That's got the mark of interference of Annie and Joan on it, Bernice thought. But who cares? I'm going.

"No," said Helen, when Bernice joked about their intervention. "I honestly did not hear anything from them. But if you were missing me, then we were sitting alone, missing each other separately." She laughed her marvelous warming laugh, and took Bernice's coat.

"Wow, you're hanging up my coat for me!"

"Well, this is the first time I think you've knocked and waited to be let in. You're always coat hung up and halfway through to the kitchen before I even know there's someone at the door!"

Bernice laughed. "I am a little bold, aren't I?"

"Yes you are, and I would not have you any other way. Sit down in the kitchen. I have just a couple more things to do and we'll be ready."

"I brought you some chickens," Bernice said, handing her a bag. "They had a nice deal on some locals, so I took it."

"Oh you're so thoughtful. I hope you didn't cut anyone out of the food group." Helen was referring to the folks whom Bernice generously provided food each week.

"No, there were many extra. In fact, if I get back in, I'll get one for Annie and Joan, too."

"Or they can just come over and join us. You girls have been shrinking Violets this month."

Bernice sat at the kitchen table. "Ah, Helen, we just don't want to intrude. We stayed pretty long after Christmas as it was."

Helen stopped her sandwich making, put her hands on her hips and said, "Bernice St. John! You girls know better than that! I was sure everyone was busy—Joan's got work, Annie's got the shop, both of them with weddings to plan, and—"

"Well. . ."

"Well what?"

"The weddings aren't exactly getting planned just yet."

"What?"

"Well, Laureen's is, she came over while I was there the other night."

"Well, I'm happy for Laureen, but what about Joan, what about Annie? What am I missing?"

"I expect you know that Sylvester's putting it off."

"Putting it off? No, I hadn't heard that. I heard that there would be a few months, maybe six."

"To hear Annie tell it, there's no date at the moment and she doesn't know when to expect one."

"Oh good heavens. Harry!" she called toward the bedroom. "Come in here, please!"

Bernice got the distinct feeling of being the good kid when someone was being called to the principal's office.

"Hello lambchop," Harry said heading for his wife with open arms.

Helen didn't deflect his kiss, but then, more calmly said, "I hear Annie's wedding has been put off. For she doesn't know how long." She didn't say anything else, just stood there staring at Harry.

Harry backed up a little, noticed Bernice and said, "Oh, hello there!"

"Harry," said Helen.

"Well, I don't really know what Sly's plans are exactly," Harry began looking from one of them to the other. "You know, maybe they're getting involved in some objective that's going to eat up more time. I really don't know, honey. Maybe I can find out." He raised his eyebrows, as if to say, is that what you wanted me to do?

Bernice felt as if she were in the midst of a covert planning session and struggled not to smile. In the end, she had to turn her face away and pretend to check something on her skirt.

Her discomfort was not lost on Helen, who decided it might be time for her to explain things, at least to Bernice. But not in front of Harry.

The sandwiches were made with Helen's homemade white bread, a thing Harry had requested she never stop making. And the roast turned out to be a tender pork shoulder, which was warmed and dressed in a nice tasty sauce that Helen had concocted.

"It's always such a treat to eat over here," Bernice said. "Thank you for asking me."

"I agree," said Harry. "And thank you for inviting me, too." The girls giggled. "But before I wear out my welcome, I have errands to do so I'll be off. Bernice, it was very nice to see you. And my dear wife, I'll miss you every moment I'm away."

Helen played along. "As will I."

He gave her a quick peck on the cheek, and he was gone.

"He's wonderful, Helen," Bernice said. "Is he always so gracious?"

"No!" Helen chuckled. "But it's sure nice to have him back home. I'll never forget those scary nights, worrying and trying to talk myself out of worrying, you girls helping, but all of us fighting the fear. I don't know if I could go through it again!"

"God willing we will not have to ever again," Bernice said, picking up the plates.

"We pray that every night," Helen said. "But it's not over yet. Not by a long shot."

"No."

"There are still so many wives, girlfriends, family members waiting, hoping, fearing."

"Yep," said Bernice. "And of course some of them are worrying and their loved ones are already home."

"I think I know what you're getting at," Helen said. "Come on, let's have some coffee in the living room. I've got fresh cream!

Later, as Bernice carried her cup to the kitchen, she sighed. "So what you're saying is number one, Sly didn't tell Annie the whole story, and number two, he and his buddy Bobby, and the whole team really are actually in danger."

"Well, no, I wouldn't say danger exactly. But they're not entirely safe. The place where they work, and even the barracks-like place where they live are both secure. But Bernice, these men are doing extremely important work. It's not beneath that ugly man and others in their army to send out assassins to eliminate the threat."

"It still sounds like danger to me."

"Maybe you're an adventuress at heart," Helen chuckled.

"Hey, maybe I am!" Bernice said, brightening. "When Henry told me about those caves over there in Italy, all that secret activity, and how heroic those guys were, I felt myself wishing I could be in on it."

"Let me see, a nun who is a nurse, who works for the military intelligence. . ." she chuckled.

"Sounds about right. The only problem is, Helen, I still don't know what I really want to do. I want to know how to save people, but most nurses are part of a hospital or maybe hired in private service. That seems too confined for me. I want to be able to go out and do things. Not be under one roof and have to constantly ask permission to do something."

"I think I understand," Helen said, joining Bernice at the sink. "You want to determine your own way."

"I guess so."

"That's rough in a way because it's hard to imagine a convent where they would allow that. They have to live by the regulations that their diocese sets, so the nuns have to kind of fall in, too."

"Do you think I could adjust to it, you know, learn to live that way?"

"I think it's how you might feel when you're older," Helen said thoughtfully. "But you might run into trouble if you try to force it. I think the opportunities you've been given by having security, money in the bank I mean, make it possible for you to accomplish what you might never have thought of doing before. Like the grocery store charity."

"Yeah."

"There may be other things down the road, too. What about nursing, are you thinking about doing that?"

"I'm still not sure. Maybe something more basic, like lifesaving or something."

"So what are you up to today?"

"I've got to check with Bob and see how things are looking at the store. He's a find, Helen. I'm so lucky."

"I'm sure he feels the same way!"

On Bernice's way to the store, she thought about the irony in how Helen was trying not to intrude on their time and the girls were trying not to intrude on her time. I wonder how many situations crop up where people get mixed up just because they misinterpret and make wrong assumptions, she thought. I bet that happens more often than we think.

Dick was also on foot, heading to his appointment with Mr. Marini. If this job turns out to be what it sounds like, he thought, I will be making the grade in no time. It's good I spent a little time brushing up on my management theory. It's been a while, and it's even been a while since I put it into practice.

A private home was a funny place to meet for an interview, Dick thought. But a lot of wealthy men didn't spend all day in their businesses. He had heard that and seen it in movies; posh homes with men in silken smoking jackets, sitting with pipes and a maid bringing coffee on a tray. He wondered if it would be that way at Mr. Marini's residence.

He paused to check the address, being unfamiliar with the area. The invitation did not describe the house, only that it was set back from the road just outside the business district. He had the address, but there were many streets whose names were not posted at the intersections, and he hoped he didn't miss it because of that. Dick had declined to take the bus into town, having become more familiar with the town, but the angled and unnamed streets were challenging him.

After a couple of blocks he came to the same main road he had traveled on foot with Joan. He would have to turn left, he decided, to go toward town, pass through it, and just beyond, look for the Marini residence. As it turned out, his navigation skills were working just fine. And only fifteen minutes later, and perfectly on time, he looked to the left to see a large stately looking residence set back from the road.

He checked the name on sign and discovered to his satisfaction that he had reached his destination. He opened the imposing, black, wrought iron gate, and began to ascend the long driveway.

Watching him read the name and then go on through the gate, mouth agape, and totally unbeknownst to Dick, was a flabbergasted Bernice St. John.

Chapter Twelve

At the Marini residence, Dick paused, mildly inhibited by its grandiose appearance. There were many such mansions on 16th Street where he had grown up, but not directly in his neighborhood, and most of those houses belonged to stately folks such as diplomats and cabinet members. He took hold of a large brass hinged knob and gave the door a good couple of knocks.

Almost instantly, it opened, and to Dick's utter amazement, a man wearing a smoking jacket stood at the door.

"Welcome," said the man. "It's nice to see you could make it."

Dick put out his hand. "Nice to meet you, Sir, I'm Dick Thimble.

"And it's nice to meet you, too," said the man, shaking his hand, "I am Bindeman, the butler."

"Oh, I, well, nice to meet you."

"As you said. Come this way, Mr. Thimble."

Dick followed the man down a short hallway, through a very large, well-lit room, and down another hallway, and into a very small room, with a modest bed, a desk, and a small window situated high on the wall.

"Please have a seat anywhere," Bindeman said.

"Well, thank you," Dick said, moving a stack of books that sat on the only chair in the room.

"I'll be back momentarily, Sir."

Dick looked around. He found it odd that an interview would be held in what looked like a servant's quarters, but perhaps, he reasoned, it was due to some problem with the other rooms. Or maybe they were converting some of the rooms into offices and hadn't finished yet. But who was he to judge? He was just there to try to get on the Marini payroll.

After a while he heard some whispering in the hall. He couldn't quite make out what was being said, but it sounded like women's voices. At least one of them was a woman. He shifted in his chair, and the whispering stopped abruptly.

He was getting a little hungry. Too nervous to eat breakfast, he had planned on stopping at the diner for maybe a hotdog or whatever was cheap before heading back home after the meeting. If he had to wait much longer, he worried that the noises his stomach produced might be audible.

Just then, Bindeman reappeared carrying a tray with coffee and little cakes, as well as what looked like neatly cut, but very small peanut butter and jelly sandwiches.

"Coffee, Sir?" Bindeman asked, setting down the tray on the bed.

"Thank you," said Dick. "Black is fine."

Bindeman handed him a cup of coffee and a plate with a sampling of what he had brought. "I hope this will be satisfactory," he said. He gave a little head bow and leaving the tray, disappeared out the door.

Well, that's one problem solved, Dick said, having some coffee and a cake. He hadn't been completely convinced that the sandwiches were peanut butter and jelly, but up close, there was no denying it. He ate one of them as well.

Just as he had finished it, a voice startled him. Standing in the doorway, was a tall, thin man in butler's garb. "I thought you'd like the peanut butter and jelly!" he cried with enthusiasm. "Aren't they just delightful?" He high-stepped into the room, as if leading a parade, and sat on the floor, cross-legged, staring up admiringly at Dick.

Dick smiled, unsure of what he was engaged in. Not a word would come to him, so the scene remained; two men smiling at each other, one on a chair, and one on the floor.

"Is there anything else, Sir?" came the voice of Bindeman from the hall. Only that time, he was addressing the man on the floor.

"Oh no, thank you Bindeman. We are having a great time, aren't we?" He looked at Dick for an answer.

"Why, uh, yes. . ."

"So Gloria says you're a fine man," said the man on the floor.

"Excuse me, Sir," Dick said. "Are you Mr. Marini?"

"Why yes I am! Oh, and you're wondering why I'm dressed like the butler? This is our switch-your-clothes day! We do this every week! Isn't that fun?"

"Oh, well I guess it is," said Dick.

"I imagine you came over to play with Gloria," Mr. Marini said.

"Well—"

"I hate to have to tell you, but she is not here! She's gone out!"

"I see, but—"

"I would play with you but it doesn't look as if you've brought any toys with you," Mr. Marini said. "I don't care for girls' toys."

Just then Dick heard the running of heeled shoes across a marble floor, then the muffled sound of them traversing the long hallway carpet, and then at the doorway appeared Gloria, her face flushed with anger and embarrassment.

"Get off that floor," she said. "Father, you'll get all dirty."

"But I'm the butler today, Gloria," he said.

"Where is Mr. Kinder?" She looked down the hall, and back at her father, and only then, regarded Dick with a kind of dark embarrassment. "I'm sorry, Dick," she said, not quite looking him in the eye. "Mr. Kinder was to hold your interview."

"Well, Gloria," Dick began.

"No, no, no, no, no!" Gloria said. "I won't have this ruined. Father, get up! Bindeman! Bindeman!"

Bindeman appeared almost by magic, and said softly, "Yes, Miss?"

"Why isn't Father, what is going on?"

"It's switching day, Miss."

"I know that, but where is Mr. Kinder? He knew I had set up an appointment!"

"I don't know, Miss."

"I think I should try again another time," Dick managed to say, as he rose and set the coffee cup and plate on the tray. "Maybe it's not convenient for Mr. uh, Mr. Kinder?"

"Oh!" said Gloria, and ran out of the room, up a set of stairs and out of sight.

"Thank you for the peanut butter jelly sandwich," Dick said to Mr. Marini, who still sat cross-legged on the floor. "It was good."

The man leaned forward conspiratorially and whispered, "Next time you come, I like the Lincoln Logs. Or the Tinker Toys. Okay?" He smiled, his eyebrows arched, and nodded repeatedly.

"Yes, indeed," said Dick.

Feeling as though there were no time like the present, Dick made a beeline for the front door, hesitating only as he got there, for there on the far side of the entry stood Gloria, appearing suddenly almost like the White Rabbit in Alice in Wonderland, he thought.

"I'm so sorry things didn't work out this afternoon," she said, once again, fully composed and completely pulled together. "Let's make it another time really soon. It was so great to see you!"

Dick nodded and opened the door. "Yes," he said, and pulled the door closed behind him. Halfway down the drive, he wondered if any of that had actually happened, or if he was just having another post-battlefield dream. When he got through the wrought iron gate, though, and felt the blast of bus exhaust fumes in his face, he decided it was real.

At just about that same time, Harry arrived at the Ft. Dix outpost and found Sly and Bobby both wrestling with decoding structure and substance studies.

"It ain't as easy as they made it out to be," Bobby complained when he saw Harry. "But it's good to see you, Cap. Or sorry, Maj."

"How are you fellows making out? You think you're going to stick with it?"

"I am," said Sly. "It's a challenge, but I like that part about it. It's a lot harder than interpreting for the interrogators and a lot less, what do they call it? Traumatic."

"That's for sure," said Bobby, shaking his head as if dispelling a vision.

"If you make it through the course okay, they'll certify you. That'll be a good thing as time goes on, trust me," said Harry.

"Well hopefully this war won't go on much longer," Sly said.

"Even after," said Harry, "as I imagine you'll start to learn as you get into the actual work of decoding."

Bobby and Sly looked at each other.

"Yeah, it's not for inexperienced guys," Harry said. "And that's why they wanted you two so badly. But listen, I got some important information."

"Is this somethin' we gotta go somewhere else for?" Sly asked, indicating the other men in the room.

"Let's get a cup of coffee at the mess," Harry said.

Later, as they huddled over coffee and sandwiches, Harry tapped his ear and mouth, to indicate it was for their ears only, and said bluntly, "There's been an attack on a decoding base in Maryland. No one was hurt, but it was clear what they were after. You won't hear about it in the news. They're calling it a boiler accident. But it was a bomb that was left in the hallway of the building where the actual work is done. They've got nothing on it yet. The detectives have taken some clues from it, but it has the mark of the Nazi sympathizers."

"What, they left swastikas?" Bobby asked.

"No, other things I can't go into. But I have to let you in on this so you know what the risks are."

"Who's going to tell them other guys?" Sly asked.

"At the barracks? I think they've already been told," Harry said. "I was coming up so I told the Security folks that I'd have a talk with you since you're new to this. If you want out, it's okay, no hard feelings, no questions asked."

"I ain't goin' nowhere," said Bobby. "But what do I tell Debbie?"

"You tell her nothing!" Harry said, his voice rising. Then remembering to keep it quiet, he repeated himself in a calmer voice. "I'm sorry, they just can't know. No one can. Not Helen, no one. As far as everyone knows, you're working on something for the Army. That's all."

Sly nodded. "This part is the hard part. I don't like keeping secrets. Not from Annie."

"Nobody does," said Bobby.

The next day, it was time for Annie's cast to be removed. It had been a long wait and she was eager to be done with the thing.

"I don't even need it," she said to Joan as Joan hurried on with her coat.

"Well, that's the point," Joan said. "If you don't need it anymore, they take it off."

Then she caught Annie mimicking her and laughed. "Well, I don't mean to be mean, but that's true isn't it?"

"Yes, it's true," said Annie. "I was just proud that I had managed to heal so well."

"Well you didn't do it," said Joan. "Your body did it. You were just an innocent bystander."

"Go to work, will ya?" Annie laughed.

Joan went to the door, "Don't break your other leg on the way there!" she called and popped out the door.

Only one more hour, Annie thought, although having a doctor appointment at eight o'clock in the morning seemed ridiculous. She would gladly have closed the shop for the appointment, but the doctor's nurse was adamant. If you want it done this week, you'll come at 8am. Regular people are still sleeping at this hour, Annie thought, helping herself to another cup of coffee.

In fact, Annie was nervous about the appointment. She had heard that sometimes bones didn't heal correctly in adult injuries. It hadn't been a bad injury, but who knew what was going on under that cast? No one had seen inside it for a long time!

"To tell you the truth, I'm scared," she said later to Bernice as she maneuvered her car out of their driveway.

"What are you scared about? You had a broken leg, it's all better now."

"So that's all there is to it?"

"What else is there?"

"There's lack of feeling, lack of movement, uneven limbs, scaly skin, malformed healing—

"Malformed healing? What is that? Is that real?"

"Well, I don't know, but I don't want to have it," Annie said.

Bernice laughed. "Either do I!"

Annie was taken right away when they arrived, since she was the first patient. Bernice sat in the waiting room thinking about what she had seen the previous day.

What in the world was he doing going to Gloria's house? Was it really over between Dick and Joan, after all they had been through together, and how far they'd come?

No part of her could believe that Dick was truly seeing Gloria, yet she could not come up with a satisfactory explanation for having seen him opening the Marini's gate and going up the driveway.

I won't tell Annie, she told herself. She'll get upset and she's got enough on her mind already. Although once she gets her cast off, a lot will be resolved.

Annie's appointment, happily, was very brief, her cast was removed, she was given instructions on what to do and what not to do, and sent on her way.

"Did you have any malformed healing?" Bernice asked.

"Shut up, Bernice," said Annie as Bernice struggled to hide her laughter. "It's fine. My leg is fine. No jokes, please."

"Yes madame, and where to now?"

"It's still early, you want to go to the diner?"

"Okay, but only if it's my treat. I'm feeling magnanimous today. Besides I want your opinion on something."

When Bernice pulled up to the diner, she saw that they were not opening until later that day due to a water problem. "I was really getting in the mood for their hashed browns," said Bernice. "Oh well. Your place?"

"Sure," said Annie. "Also your treat?"

"No, yours!" Bernice said.

At Annie's, they had left over coffee and day-old toast, warmed in the oven. "I'm the last of the big spenders," Annie said, bringing the toast to the table. "But I've got a sugar and cinnamon shaker if you like that."

"Oh I do, give it to me!" said Bernice. "Where do you get a thing like that?"

"I got mine at the variety store," Annie said. "I think they have them at Kresge's too."

After a while, Bernice having thought it over, decided maybe she would bring up the subject. "Annie," she said, as if she were about to make an announcement, "I saw something that's puzzling and disturbing."

Annie's eyes lit up. "Oh, do tell!" she said. "I love puzzles."

"It's not that kind. In fact, it's more disturbing than puzzling."

"Okay. So animal, mineral, or vegetable?"

"What?"

"Well, if we're going to play 20 Questions, I'd like to get started."

"Okay, okay. I saw somebody—oh this feels like gossip! But it's not Annie. I really am confused by it."

Annie spoke through clenched teeth. "You're confused by what already?"

"I'm sorry. Yesterday, as I was walking to the store, I came upon Dick coming from the opposite direction, and turning, and of this I am positive, into the Marini gate and going up the driveway." She paused. "What do you make of that?"

Annie stared hard at her. "Are you sure it was Dick?"

"Of course I am!"

"Well people don't just go in there. They say the old man requires some kind of vetting of visitors or something like that."

"So maybe he had a vetting. By the way, what is a vetting?"

"Well maybe he was there to see, well, you know who."

"That's what I think. I don't see why though. I mean what in the world did Joanie say to him anyway?"

"You know, Bernice, I wasn't there, but when she came home, she was hopping mad. Then before maybe an hour passed, she was changing her tune. The next day, she knew she'd made a big mistake, but she doesn't have any way to contact him, so she's really twisted up about this. She's trying to put it out of her mind, like we did before Christmas, but this is so different."

Bernice sat back and sighed. "I just don't see how a man that good, who was that much in love with Joan, could throw it all away over one little fight."

"One big fight."

"Yeah, one big fight."

"Me either. I think maybe. . . I don't know." Annie shook her head. "I'm drawing a blank. Any other time, I can think of reasons that explain things, but not this."

"Me neither. By the way, guess who invited me to lunch yesterday, thank you very much!"

"Huh?"

"Don't tell me you and Joan didn't tell Helen I was missing her."

"We didn't! Honest! Not unless Joanie wrote her a card or something."

"Well, Helen said she was missing us as much as we were missing her. We had a good laugh over that one. It was so good to be with her and laugh and everything."

"I'm jealous."

"Well, what do you say we go see her now, breakfast ought to be over for everybody. We can just stop in and maybe you two can catch up."

"I got no problem with that."

"Can your malformation handle the walk, or do you want to go in the car?"

"Walk."

They enjoyed the walk, talking and laughing along the way, just as they had done before, when the men were still away. It was good to get back to walking together. Especially with no cast, as far as Annie was concerned.

Bernice opened Helen's door and started to walk in, and Annie grabbed her arm and hissed at her, "Bernice! What if they're kissing or something. . ."

"Oh!" Bernice immediately stepped back outside. "I forgot about Harry! We were just walking like old times and—"

"Well, hello stranger!" said Helen. "Bernice, why are you now knocking instead of just coming in?"

"I was just thinking about old times—"

Helen looked perplexed.

"She means she forgot Harry. Harry is home now so maybe the door deserves to be knocked on when we stop by, especially without warning."

Helen laughed merrily. "Our days of romance in the middle of the day are probably past us," she finally said. "But thank you for making me realize you think of us as a couple of honeymooners!"

"See?" said Bernice to Annie.

"Oh, as if you knew!" said Annie.

"Hey, no cast!" said Helen. "Isn't that nice! When did that happen?"

"About an hour ago," said Bernice. "She narrowly escaped malformed healing."

"What?" said Helen, walking into the kitchen. "Let's all sit down."

"She means I'm fine," Annie said, taking a seat and making a face at Bernice. "Bernice is confused."

"You are?" Helen said to Bernice. "Would coffee help?"

"We're spoiled today on coffee," said Bernice. "But yes, it would."

Helen laughed and got back up to pour them some coffee and get out the cream. "I was thrilled when they increased the coffee ration. Feels like a luxury! So tell me why you're confused."

"It's not a big mystery, Bern, just spill it."

"All right. I'm confused about why I saw Dick Thimble open the Marini family estate gate and walk up the driveway yesterday."

Helen stopped in mid-pour. "Did I hear you correctly? Dick was going to Gloria's house? I didn't even know he was back in town."

"Either did I, come to think of it," said Annie.

"Me neither!" said Bernice, looking at Annie. "But he was headed to her house, and we can't think of one good reason why."

"Was he with anyone else?"

"No. When I saw him, it looked like he was reading an address from maybe a slip of paper or something. He put it back in his pocket after he looked at it, and that's when he opened the gate and went in."

"Well, girls," Helen said, putting her hands on her hips. "I can't think of a single good reason why he would be doing something like that either."

Chapter Thirteen

Harry stood and put on his jacket. "It was great to see you men," he said. "Feels like old times."

"Better than old times," Bobby said. "Good to see you too, Sir."

They shook hands. "You don't have to call me "sir" anymore," Harry said. "But you can!" He started to laugh.

Just at that moment, they heard shots, loud fire just outside. It sounded nearby. The three of them responded immediately, cooperating in tandem as if they'd never left the battle front. Harry looked out the entry door, side arm poised, and Sly and Bobby investigated at the windows and rear door. Harry yelled at the others in the mess to get down. They responded immediately.

Harry opened the door cautiously after seeing the back of a man fleeing on foot into the surrounding woods. "Sly, call the MPs. I think I saw the sniper."

Bobby yelled, "Hey Cap, over here! Help me get him in." Just outside the rear door, an injured guard lay unconscious, bleeding from the abdomen.

"It don't look good," Sly said later as they waited for the medical personnel. "I got pressure on it, but that was fired at close range."

Harry was stewing, pacing back and forth. "How did someone just pop up out of the woods, completely undetected and shoot a guard!" he demanded.

"Well, at least you got a glimpse, and you seen where he went," Bobby said. "They'll get him. And when they do, I'm guessing we'll get some answers."

"Yeah, what the hell?" said Sly. "Is this some kind of international, organized thing?"

"I came up here to tell you about the Maryland attack just to make you aware but I sure didn't think there was any real danger. And now this. These guys are probably trying to intimidate the nonmilitary personnel because we're pulling ahead."

"Yeah, gettin' desperate. But they ain't doing much intimidating running around on foot with a handgun in the middle of a military installation!" Bobby said.

"Maybe not, but they shot someone," Sly said. "And look at those guys over there. They don't look too pleased."

"Nah, they're not intimidated. Angry maybe."

"Whatever their intention," Harry said, still pacing, "we gotta disrupt it soon, or somebody better."

"They'll pull you right back into active duty if you keep talkin' like that, Major Ashenbach," Bobby chuckled.

"Oh, Helen'll love that!" Sly said.

"How long they gonna keep this place on lock down anyway?" Harry said, frustrated.

Military Police stood at each door, which kept the civilians calm, and maintained order. Outside, they stood watch at the doors and another group patrolled the perimeter, searching for evidence. Harry had given as detailed a report as he could. His nonmilitary status kept him from joining the investigation. The thought of standing by, unable to act, was starting to get to him.

"He's like a lion in the zoo," Bobby said to Sly under his breath.

"Poor guy. He's still in Intelligence," Sly agreed, "whether he knows it or not."

The MPs' commander entered the building then and quietly gave some orders to the patrols at the doors. Then he cleared his throat, and spoke to everyone in a loud voice. "If I could have your attention please. We've completed our search of the premises, and whoever is responsible for the attack on Patrolman Schultz has escaped. However, we've been able to put together a few clues. For the time being, we will be maintaining the guards outside this mess and commissary, and throughout the base. It's essential that we all stay on alert, and notify an MP if they see something that looks suspicious or out of the ordinary. Thank you. Is Major Harry Ashenbach still here?"

Harry immediately joined the commander, eager to learn whatever he could.

"Here we go," said Sly. "Now it's not just us in this. No way he'll be able to resist. At least when the girls find out, we'll be a band of three."

Bobby snickered. "That ain't gonna help, brother." He shook his head. "I'm not liking this."

"The secrecy? Neither am I."

Helen was no spring chicken, and Harry's sudden interest in Sly and Bobby's jobs had left her feeling at loose ends. She knew her husband. He and she had been enjoying a marvelous getting-to-know-you-again time since he'd returned from Italy on Christmas. She found him just as attractive and interesting of a man at her age as she had when she was a young girl.

But she'd also come to know him better. And she knew that there was very little she could do to dissuade Harry from getting involved if he thought he could serve in some capacity.

Not that she had a leg to stand on. Helen was very much the same way. Her work for the church and even at the hospital over the last few years was legendary. She had inspired the girls to help at one event years before, they also had given their time and talent ever since.

She also knew that there was some information about these "jobs" the boys had that she was not given. So much of what Harry had done over the preceding years in the War had been on a need-to-know only basis. Helen did not need to know any of it, as far as the Army was concerned.

But she could sense things. And she wasn't alone.

Annie tapped on her door. "Hi Helen!" she called.

"Come on in, Annie!"

"Ever since I got my legs back today, I haven't stopped walking!"

Helen laughed. "Did you open the shop?"

"Nope, I never did. Listen, is Harry coming back for dinner, or are you free?"

"I don't know, but I think he's going to be late. It's a long drive up there. Why do you ask?"

"We thought it would be fun to have a girls night out, sort of put aside our cares and spend some time together at the diner."

"Great idea," said Helen. "When did you want to go?"

"I guess around six or so. We'll come by and we can all walk down together."

"That sounds nice. We can wear headlamps."

Annie laughed.

They might as well have worn headlamps. The night was pitch dark, a clouded sky and no moon, no streetlights.

"I'm starting to grow cat's eyes," Joan said as they walked along. "I swear I can see almost as well in the dark as I can in the light."

"Yeah, like the root children," said Bernice.

"Like the what?" said Annie.

"Root children, you know, the ones that run around under the earth, and play among the roots and dirt and stuff."

"I didn't know about them," Annie said. "Are they nice kids?"

Helen laughed.

"I never met one, smarty pants," said Bernice. "But I'm guessing they'd be reasonably nice."

"I agree," said Joan. "Did they have fertilizing duties, Bernice? Like helping the roots and stuff?"

"I think they were too young for that," Bernice answered.

"The only roots I know about," said Helen, are these grey ones I have to keep covering up. Maybe I should just give up and go grey."

"But would you?" said Annie. "Ma says if she didn't cover the ugly greys that she would be half and half."

"Gee, I don't know," said Helen. "That's a good point."

"What does Harry say?" Joan asked.

"Harry? I would never ask him in a million years!" Everybody laughed.

"Did you leave him a note?" Joan asked.

"Yes, I did," said Helen. "I didn't want him to worry." She paused. "See, that's where we're different!"

Everyone laughed again.

"It must be nice having him home now, though," Joan went on. "He was gone for so long."

"It really is. But of course it's good to keep a balance on things. This night out is fun and keeps me from feeling like the one left behind when he goes out. It was a really good idea, girls. Thank you."

"Are you kidding?" Annie said. "Bernice was crying in her pillow because we didn't all get together anymore."

"Unless you got eyes like Joan, you can't see me," said Bernice, "but I'm making a very mean face at you."

Joan giggled. "I can see it!"

Inside the diner and seated at their favorite booth, although unable to look out at the night due to the blackout conditions, the group sat comfortably studying the menu.

"Get whatever you like, girls. Bernice is paying," Annie said.

"You think I'm not?" Bernice said. "I am paying, and everyone except Annie should get what they want. Annie, you can have a glass of water and a crust of bread."

"Sounds yummy!" giggled Joan.

"I don't think Bernice should have to pay," Helen said.

"I don't have to, I want to," Bernice insisted. "Gives me energy."

"Oh?"

"You know that song, don't you? It's just like a magic penny; hold it tight and you don't have any. But if you spend it you'll have so many they'll roll all over the floor," she sang.

"That's such a nice sentiment!" Joan said. "And I for one and all for it!"

"It's so good to see you happy," Helen said squeezing Joan's hand.

Joan smiled. "I got faith. I know I acted badly, but I believe I will get a chance to make things right. And until then, what's the sense of moping around? It's not possible when I'm with you three anyway, so why try?"

"Absolutely," said Helen.

They were quiet for a few minutes, happily studying the menu, when the waitress appeared. "What'll ya have?"

Annie was startled. "Oh, hello. I think we're still looking," she said.

"I'll be back," said the waitress, and flew silently to another table.

"We shoulda asked what's the special," Joan said.

"You shoulda asked where Dick's been spending his time," came a painfully familiar redheaded voice.

Four heads jerked up from their menus to see Gloria, decked out in winter white from head to toe. She wore a white fur jacket with a slinky white wool dress and white muff. Her curls were entwined with strands of pearls, and she wore a white fur tam.

No one answered.

Gloria looked at Joan. "Cat got your tongue?" she said.

"No," said Bernice. "She has cat eyes."

Annie stifled a giggle.

"Hello, Gloria, how are you?" Helen said, silently praying that by being civil to her, they could get her to keep quiet about Dick's visit to her house. "I haven't seen you for a while."

"We should be so lucky," Annie said under her breath.

"Well," said Gloria, holding out her left hand and admiring a ring that adorned her finger, "I've been around. But most recently, I've had the good fortune of seeing a good friend of yours," she looked at Joan. "Dick Thimble decided to pay me a visit this morning."

"Huh?" Joan said. Wait, she thought, Dick isn't even here in town, or is he? Did he really go and see her? And why is she flashing that ring? Her mind was on instant overload trying to figure out what to think and then what to say.

Helen was tongue-tied, not having prepared any kind of response. But Bernice was not.

"Go sit down, Gloria," she said. "We're having a private gathering."

"Well, I'm sure that's how it is for women in your situation," Gloria snarled. "That's a good idea, call it 'private,' then you can avoid the title of 'old maid.'"

Annie tried to get up, but she was seated on the inside of the booth and Bernice blocked her. "Let me at her!" she cried. "I'll kill her!"

"You better get out of here," Bernice said.

Gloria looked startled, not expecting such a dramatic response. She teetered down the long aisle of booths and sat down with another one of her series of escorts.

"You shoulda let me slug her," Annie said.

"It wouldn't have done any good," said Helen. "Oh Joan."

Joan was near tears. "Do you think it's true? And why was she waving that ring around?"

"I don't know anything about the ring," Bernice said. "It's probably just another one of her nasty tricks."

"Well, what about Dick? Do you think he came up here to see her?" Joan said. "Just her. Not me?"

"Listen Joan, I did see something. I don't know why or the circumstances or anything, but when I was on my way to the grocery today, I saw Dick going through the gate that leads to her place. It could have been anything. Maybe she asked him to drop something off, or maybe she had, I don't know, information about an apartment or—"

"Or maybe he had a date?" Joan said, the tears coming. "Or maybe they decided to pick up where he and I left off, since I'm such a miserable, jealous, unattractive nag?"

Helen put an arm around her, trying to calm her down. "I'm sure it was nothing, Joan. Dick loves you."

Annie jumped in. "Of course he does. He's not interested in that old clothes horse. He's proven that over and over again."

Joan stopped crying and looked at them all wide-eyed. "Yes, he's proven it over and over, and he's tired of having to. He's moved on to someone who has always been there waiting." She got up to leave. "I can't eat. I'm sorry. I have to go."

"Well then we're all going with you," said Helen. "Come on, we're going to my house."

Gloria watched from a distance, as the four of them gathered their coats and streamed out of the diner, not having ordered a thing. She looked at the ring on her hand given to her by her mother when she had turned sixteen. She smiled a very unattractive smile.

At that very moment, Dick was considering describing his unusual visit to Bob. At the stove, Bob was heating up the last of a concoction he had put together a few days before.

"I'm not very good at this reheating business," he said. "Seems like I always end up burning things."

"Turn it on low," Dick said. "Keep it low and do something else. It'll drive you crazy to wait for it."

"That's probably why I burn things."

"I decided to visit Gloria's father and see what it was all about," Dick said quickly.

Bob turned his head with a jerk. "You're kidding!" he said. "I thought you were listening to reason."

"I might have saved myself a little embarrassment if I had," Dick said. "I'm just glad I never mentioned it to Joan."

Bob put the pot on low and joined Dick at the table. "Dodged a bullet there, huh? Okay, tell me what happened," he said, "since you went ahead anyway, you nit wit."

"I'm telling you, Bob, that has got to be the oddest experience of my life. It was like something in a movie."

"Okay, okay, what happened?"

"This fellow answers the door in a smoking jacket."

"Well, that's what they do, the rich guys. At least in the movies."

"Yeah. Well that's what I thought. But after I introduced myself, he introduced himself as Bindeman, the butler."

"Huh?"

"Yeah, and he takes me through a bunch of rooms and for some reason, we end up in this small bedroom."

"Bedroom? For an interview?"

"It gets better. Then, as I'm waiting, I hear a kind of funny scuffle in the hall, and the butler comes back, and he puts down a tray of among other things, peanut butter and jelly sandwiches. Cut really small though."

By that time, Bob was sitting and laughing. "Go on."

"Okay, so I'm waiting, and I was hungry. I went ahead and had a sandwich. And then suddenly from the hall, I hear a voice going, 'glad you liked the sandwich,' or something like that, and this other fellow comes in wearing a butler's uniform, and sits on the floor."

"On the floor?"

"Yeah, cross-legged."

Bob was starting to roar. "Go on!" he said.

"Well, I come to find out after a few questions that he's Mr. Marini. Yes, the guy sitting on the floor. I waited for a while, and he kind of giggled at me a little and then finally said, 'You're hear to play with Gloria, aren't you?' Well, I hardly knew what to say to that. I was starting to get that this guy was missing a few, you know, cards out of the deck. And in comes Gloria and says 'Father, get off the floor,' Boy was she fired up. She disappears and he asks me if I've brought any toys. He doesn't like girl toys. I told him I thought it was time for me to go, and he was alright with that, but he asked me next time I came to bring Lincoln Logs or Tinker Toys."

Bob was trying to catch his breath, wiping his eyes with the dishtowel. "Is this for real, or are you pulling my leg?"

"Every word of it is true," Dick said. "I felt I had to get out of there. If someone is that far gone, you never know what they might try to do."

"Well so," Bob said puffing, and trying not to laugh, "do you think you got the job?"

Chapter Fourteen

Margaret soon-to-be Blank strode into Annie's shop the next morning, looking as much as Margaret could look, like an excited bride. "I'm a very excited bride," she said.

Annie smiled. She had long come to understand that Margaret's method of expression always seemed to underline the facts but didn't quite come across with any of the usual expression of emotion. "I'm sure you are!" she responded. "I'm so happy for you! Have you and Elwood set a date yet?"

"We'll be wed very soon," she said, "but the actual date of the occasion is not yet determined."

"Are you waiting to hear from relatives?"

"No. The relatives will have to bandy around our schedule. We are hoping to secure the church and the hall, for our reception. But since the War started, date setting has become difficult."

"Well, and you would know," said Annie, meaning that Margaret was the church secretary, with first-hand knowledge of how things were being run.

"Well, I'm the secretary. It's my job, of course."

"Yes," said Annie.

"I'll tell you what brings me here today. I'm a very excited bride, here to ask you to be a bride's maid."

Annie nodded. She was happy for Margaret, whom she had always had her doubts would find a husband. Yet here she was, being married before Annie or Joan, or possibly even Laureen, who had been engaged longer than all of them. And Margaret had not changed a thing about herself. She still wore the clompy shoes she had always worn, her bobbed hair and glasses, face free of makeup and plain clothing all remained the same. Yet she had found, ironically through Annie's assistance, an apparently perfect match for herself.

It had been only a few months since Annie had enjoyed wandering the wards of the mobile GIs, scanning the beds for men who might be good prospects for unusual but reliable and good-hearted Margaret. Her discovery of Sgt. Elwood Blank had been miraculous. When Annie had introduced them, their relationship took like wildfire, and soon they were almost inseparable.

Aside from his very deadpan manner and concern for his men, Elwood remained a mystery to Annie. She wondered suddenly if he would be returned to the field once he recovered from his injuries.

"Well, if you require time to make your decision, I'd be willing to wait a specified measure of time," Margaret was saying. "Perhaps a two-week period?"

"Oh no," said Annie. "I'm sorry, I was just thinking about how lucky you are, and wondering—"

"No, I believe entering into marriage with another has no element of luck in it. In other words, I don't feel one should leave anything to chance. Elwood agrees."

"Oh of course not, no," said Annie. "No, one needs to be sure."

"You're reversing your statement then?"

"I think I might have used the wrong word to begin with," Annie said, wishing she hadn't. "I meant I'm happy for you, I guess."

"Well that's different. Thank you."

"Will Elwood be returning to his unit?"

"No. His injury wasn't so bad that he couldn't, but he will be going to school for a new type of computing or something, and it will involve quite a lot of time. The school is in Texas, and as I understand it, I will not be allowed to tag along."

"Oh, I'm sorry."

"Thank you. It will be a hardship. But we have discussed it and we will manage. I'll continue to live at home until we can relocate together."

"After the war is over?"

"Whatever comes."

Annie was startled by Margaret's sudden philosophical statement. What was in her mind, she wondered, this girl who expressed herself so emotionlessly? She wanted to say that certainly she would be her bride's maid, but Margaret was already at the door.

"Let me know!" she said, and she disappeared.

Margaret now, too, Annie thought. After the disaster at the diner last night, I hope she doesn't approach Joan. It's no surprise though. We all knew they were engaged. Still, after Gloria had dropped her bombshell about dating, or at least "seeing" Dick, Joan had become very removed.

How, Annie wondered, could such a seemingly perfectly matched couple come to so much harm in so short a period? Was it true what Gloria had said? It had to be, considering Bernice had seen him going into her house. Well, not the house, just the gate. Maybe he'd stopped and turned around? Now I'm grasping at straws! But what on earth was he seeing her about anyway? He didn't care for her, Annie just knew it.

Just then, Bernice popped in. "Was that Margaret I saw?" she asked.

"Yes, and it's a good thing she didn't catch sight of you," Annie said, jokingly referring to Margaret's long-time misunderstanding regarding Bernice and Margaret's former boyfriend of sorts. Bernice had never had an interest in the fellow, but Margaret could not be convinced. Even now with Elwood, and despite her earlier declarations of forgiveness, she still regarded Bernice as an imposition at best.

"I kept hid around the corner 'til she made her exit," Bernice said.

"No you didn't!" Annie laughed.

"I did slow down. I could tell she wasn't coming my way, but I moderated my pace just the same."

"Aren't you supposed to be training Bob at the store?"

"Bob's a whiz. He's already training me. He's showing me ways that we can hold onto our program, but not lose money, like we've been doing. You know

Annie, I don't think I'm strong on organizational skills," she laughed.

"No, that's a tough one."

"You know how to run a shop."

"Yeah, this shop. But there are nowhere near the different things here that there are in a grocery store, even a small grocery store."

Bernice was walking around, admiring the displays Annie had put together. "These angels are beautiful," she said. "I like where you have them, too, up above. I love this place."

"Thanks."

"When does Joan get home?"

"Joan didn't go to work today."

"Oh," Bernice sighed and shook her head. "It must be devastating to learn that your fiancé has started playing the field. I don't know, Annie."

"I don't think he has."

"Well, you heard Gloria."

"I've heard Gloria before," Annie said, "and most of what she says is . . . untrue."

"You getting ready to close?" Bernice asked.

"Yeah, I just came in to finish some bookwork. I hated leaving Joan but I think she wanted to be alone anyway."

"Well, I think it's time we descended on her," Bernice said. "We gotta stick together."

"Yeah, let's get going."

Meanwhile, Dick was on the bus again. He was careful to stand away from any single women, and intent on getting to the bottom of his troubles.

His conversation that afternoon with Father Bertrand had done a lot to ease his mind. Originally,

Dick had planned to consult the priest on his relationship with Joan. He knew that Joan was very fond of Father Bertrand and felt that he might be able to give him some guidance.

To his surprise, the priest wisely declined to discuss Joan with him, but did offer some advice in general. Don't allow another person's emotions to take you off your course, especially if those emotions are uninformed or misinformed. Always remember your goal, and you can take your time, but don't change your life around to suit the feelings of the day.

In fact, Dick had been mixed up, moving away from his heart of hearts just to achieve an ancillary goal of earning money. Bob had been right, and he should have listened to him. At least he had averted disaster, not having told Joan about it. Maybe someday he would, he thought, but not soon!

His mind traveled back to a time before the War and while he and Bob had been in school together. They were both intellectually gifted; Bob with numbers, Dick with words. Back then Dick had begun to take an interest in the law, but before he'd checked into it, their service years had come. Now, the opportunity presented itself again.

Law would mean continuing to struggle for at least another three years as he worked on his degree. And he would not in good conscience be able to buy a home. There would only be enough money to rent and make the barest of essentials. But afterwards, he would be able to work a good job. The government would provide most of what he needed for the schooling. But he would still need to work.

The pieces began to fall into place. Bob's offer of work at the store was a good one. If he could apply to the law college at State, he would be able to take the bus there from Bob's apartment, and work after classes and on days off from school. Homework though. It would be long days, and probably late nights. But the idea of working toward the exciting goal of a law career, although hard work and sacrifice, was exciting to Dick, and he sat, trying to assemble all of the requirements for it in his mind. He'd need to apply soon. He might not get accepted, but he thought his chances were good. It was a good time to be a first-year law student since many of those he would compete against were still overseas. It felt almost disloyal to be grateful for that, but he had contributed, he reasoned, and he hoped to contribute to his comrades in arms when he was more qualified to do so.

As a lawyer, he could — just then, his thoughts were interrupted by the conversation between two older women entering the bus.

"Yessuh, he a help us so muchuh. My a son, he a getta bad ahurt, no? And thissa lawyer man, he fix. He a helpuh me getta the money. Now my boy, he canna have what he need," said the first woman.

"Yes, he's a good man," the other woman said. "There aren't too many around, but he's a good fellow."

Dick stopped his logistics figuring, being suddenly chilled by the conversation he had just witnessed, feeling as if God had sent the two women just to help guide him in his decision. It was all too perfect.

He looked at them, smiled and nodded. They nodded back.

"Issa gumbah?" the first one said to the other.

"I don't think so, but he's a nice looking," she answered.

They giggled in soft, ribbony laughter that only the elderly can do, and gave Dick a little wave as he stood to get off at his stop.

He smiled back, sighed, and walked home on a cloud of reignited inspiration.

Striding into the apartment, he went straight to his room and began to pack an overnight bag.

Bob had come in a few minutes earlier. "What you up to?" he asked.

"Bob, I think I know what I'm going to do," he said. "I had a great conversation with Father Bertrand, and I think I've got myself back on track. Remember how we talked about law school before we signed up?"

"Law school, yeah, but Dick—"

"Oh, I know, it's a hard road."

"Not only that, it might mean waiting with all your other plans."

"I don't know where my plans are going with my personal life," Dick said. "I know I want to marry Joan, and deep down, I think she wants to marry me. I don't know how soon all of that will work out, but right now, I want to move toward what I know will be my right path."

"Is that law school?"

"That's law school."

"Okay, so why are you packing?"

"Oh, I'm just putting together an overnight bag. I figure I'll take the bus from Atlantic City to D.C. and get the rest of what I can carry—"

"Oh no you won't," said Bob. "I'm drivin' ya, we'll go round trip and have all your stuff back here before tomorrow morning."

As Bob and Dick traveled down old Route 40 toward Washington, D.C., Annie and Bernice opened the door to Annie and Joan's house to see Joan cleaning the kitchen.

"Hi Joanie, the troublemakers are here," Annie called, putting away their coats.

"What are you doing?" Bernice asked. "You've already got the cleanest kitchen in the East."

"I thought it would be nice to get some of the greasy spots off the wall behind here," she said, indicating the stove. "It gets all sticky if you leave it."

"You need any help?" Annie asked.

"No, I'm just about done. What are you two up to?"

"Nothing much." Annie wanted to know if Margaret had invited Joan to be a bride's maid, but she didn't want to ask her, and bring the subject up without needing to. So she looked in the pantry to see what was available to eat.

"I've got the hamburger casserole in the oven," Joan said. "It'll be ready pretty soon."

"Gosh, I know, and that's darn nice of you," Annie said. "But I'm so hungry."

Bernice shook her head. "Why don't you guys let me add you to my list?"

"It's not pride, I'll tell you that," Joan said. "We get so many extras from Annie's family. It seems unfair to be taking food that could go to people who have no means to buy it. We both have incomes."

"But you're both stick figures," Bernice said, causing Annie and Joan both to start laughing. "I worry about the influence of the next nor'easter carrying you guys away. Both of you!"

"I admit I'm pretty tired of being hungry all the time. It's not essentials that we're wanting though, is it Joanie?"

"No," Joan agreed. "It's crackers and fruit pies."

"And bread, hot out of the oven whenever you turn around. I think I'm missing Ma's kitchen, to tell you the truth," Annie said. "She would be in there making something all the time—little meat pies, pepperoni bread, cheese bread with that egg wash and parmesan—that's what I miss. There was always something to eat."

"And grahams, I love grahams," Joan said.

"Graham crackers go to the soldiers. I heard that's a fact," Bernice said. "They travel well apparently."

"Well good. It's something we can offer up," Joan said.

"Yeah, whether we wanna or not!" Annie said, laughing lightly.

"How about if I at least bring a chicken over, maybe once a week?" Bernice insisted. "Considering how often I eat over, it's only fair. Remember how we pooled our food before over at Helen's? We could do that here."

"If you promise to stay and eat, I think that's a good compromise," Annie said.

"Yeah, okay," said Joan. "You said that like Margaret, Annie!" she chuckled.

Annie and Bernice stopped short.

"What?" said Joan. "I didn't mean any offense."

"Oh no, it's not that," Annie said, "it's just that—"

"Oh, yeah," Joan interrupted. "Yes, she was by today and yes, she asked me to be a bride's maid. And yes, it was a little jarring, but Margaret deserves to be happy. I don't really understand her very well, but I'm fond of her, and to tell you the truth, I'm impressed."

"You mean with her engagement?" Bernice asked.

"Yes, that she was the one who managed to form a relationship, develop trust, and determine the course of action."

"Now you sound like her!" Annie laughed.

"I know!" Joan said. "Maybe she knows something we don't."

"That don't mean you're both going to start talking like robots now, does it?" Bernice asked.

"Not me," said Annie. "I may be a dark horse, but I'm coming to the finish line."

"And when will that be?" Bernice asked.

"I don't know, but I'm coming!" Annie said.

Joan laughed. "You and Laureen both," she said.

"And you," said Annie.

"Let's stay away from that subject," Joan said. "Oh, look at the clock! Dinner's ready!"

After dinner, Joan washed the dishes, taking her time as she did so. Her dishes were not quite as delicate or expensive as Helen's, but she loved them just the same. They were white with sunflowers around the rim, and a rolling field on the inside. The cups had the face of a large sunflower seemingly open at the bottom of the cup with its long petals reaching up all around to the rim of the cup, while the saucers had beautiful circles of greenery arranged to show when the cup was sitting on top. The set of four place settings had been given to her by her mother. Annie was always relieved when Joan wanted to wash up for fear of having that one slippery soapy accident and dropping and cracking one of them.

Joan reviewed the films in her mind of getting those dishes and how she and her mother had both loved them so. It had been so long since she had seen her mother. Her parents had gone to visit friends in Indiana and ended up buying a place there. They had always intended to return, with a plan to rent out the newer place, but so far that had not happened. The sad times were when she missed her mother the most. Like Annie, her mother could always make her laugh and get perspective.

But that evening, she managed to think only of happy times, said a prayer of thanks for not feeling overcome by the situation, whatever the situation was. In actuality, Joan was not at all sure that Dick had dated Gloria. She once again, had been ready to believe the worst, a practice she hoped to change in time. But thinking it over, and seeing Margaret in her very non-emotional way manage to convey that Dick and she were meant to be together, Joan had begun to feel optimistic.

But she didn't want to talk about it. Her thoughts and responses to them were still forming, and delicate, like a child growing in the womb. She didn't want anything or anyone's opinions disturbing them. She counted her blessings to have friends like Annie and Bernice, and Helen, too, who respected her wishes not to discuss it just then.

As she finished the last of the dishes that night, she felt the presence of a peaceful being there with her, keeping her calm and moving ahead. As long as I keep busy, she told herself, I can go on. I can figure out what I'm to do. But oh, please, I don't want to be back out there, looking for someone again! The thought of joining the young women at dances and socials, looking for someone was heart-wrenching. It wasn't only because of the awful nerves it aroused, but because her heart ached for the man she already knew she loved. Allowing that love to falter might not even be possible, but if it were, she wasn't ready for it. Not yet. No matter what she knew or heard, she just could not believe that Dick was out of her life.

She was relieved at least to be alone. With Annie and Bernice talking about their shops in the other room, she welcomed the privacy. She took a deep breath, and instead of fearing the worst, she started gently singing.

Chapter Fifteen

The next day, Joan did go to work, fearing the dreaded pink slip if she stayed home another day. The morning was numbingly cold, but by the afternoon, the weather had turned slightly and it being payday, Joan got off the bus in town to go to the bank, cash her paycheck, and take a small portion with her to Kresge's. She had seen a pretty piece of fabric the previous week and thought it would make a nice blouse.

After she finished her business at the bank, being careful to set enough aside for her bills and share of the food money, she headed toward the dime store. It was a pleasant walk, the sun on her shoulders and thoughts of floral prints on her mind.

At the same time, Dick Thimble, freshly back and fully loaded into his apartment with Bob decided it was a perfect day to hoof it into town and find a nice gift for his mother's birthday. Her favorite pastime was crocheting, and he knew just the place to find some colorful yarn. Not realizing that advanced crochet-ers tend to choose their own colors, he had decided that like a painter, she might want a kind of variety pack.

Not surprisingly, seeing the tall handsome figure of Dick Thimble stride by as she was trying on shoes at the exclusive department store, Gloria quickly decided that she needed something in one of the stores that lay in the direction Dick was headed. She shoved the shoes into the box herself, yelled "Charge it!" to the salesman from across the room, and hightailed it onto the sidewalk before Dick was out of sight. Whether she would catch up to him and chat on the street, or follow him into the store, she wasn't sure. It would depend on which store he entered.

By then, Joan had made her way down the long aisle to the end rows of fabric. She traveled blissfully into a creative heaven, breezing through the beautiful bolts of fabric in rows high and low, their rich textures draped from the shelves, and varied from plain white cotton blousing to dark navy worsted wools.

The print that had caught her eye before was still there, and it looked even more beautiful than she had remembered. She felt carefree and happy as she pulled it from the shelf, moved to the nearby mirror and looked at it against her face. The colors were beautiful, but on close examination, she wasn't sure that they were flattering for her.

But there were so many others, she wasn't bothered by it. She felt the freshness in the fabrics, the brilliance of the colors, and breathed in the scents of the many and varied cottons. Just to the right of the fabric she'd remembered, she spotted another with a cream background, rich tropical greens and violet and orange blossoms.

The sight of it transported her from the cold of winter into the warmth and promise of springtime, even summer. Eagerly grabbing the bolt off the shelf, she raised the fabric to her face to test the compatibility at the nearby mirror.

Yes, that was much better, she decided happily. She draped it over her shoulder to test the weight, making sure it was not too heavy for a blouse. As she looked up at it, she noticed in the mirror, the distant reflections of two people standing face to face in the yarn department way up front. They seemed to be excited about something.

She looked down at the fabric admiring it and trying to decide if she should spend the money for the two and one-half yards she would need. She already had the pattern, and the little flowers were the perfect size for the sleeves and the little cuff at the end. She could practically see the blouse on her.

She looked up again at the mirror, having made up her mind to buy it, but just wanting to see it again. The two people were still standing there. The man wasn't gesturing much, but the woman seemed like a mad woman. She was waving her head around and waving her arms, and it almost seemed as if she were pointing at Joan.

Joan chuckled softly thinking that's the kind of thing a redhead would do, it's just like the way Gloria. . . Her mind skipped a second. She looked in the mirror again. It was Gloria. And to her shock, the man was Dick!

Joan stood there, open mouthed, transfixed by what appeared to be some sort of one-sided argument, with Gloria doing everything but handstands to make her points. Because of the distance and the other shoppers' conversations, she could not hear what was being said, but if she squinted, she could see that Dick wasn't saying anything, and only occasionally lifting his hand to try to calm Gloria.

In typical Gloria style, the angry redhead stomped out of the store, leaving Dick shaking his head. A couple of older female shoppers pushed their baskets slowly by him, in order to get a good look at what all the commotion was about. Joan herself, could not stop staring.

Just as she realized that Gloria actually had been pointing at her, Dick looked in her direction, and there she was, her back to him, staring at him in the mirror. Joan was paralyzed as their eyes met in the mirror. So this is what a stroke feels like, she thought.

Slowly she turned around to see him in real life, there inside the store with her, but aisles and aisles away. They stared at each other for what seemed like half an hour, but was only about ten seconds.

Dick was so ashamed by Gloria's wild tirade, he simply could not face Joan. First Joan erupted at him about Gloria, and next Gloria exploded at him about Joan. He didn't mind Gloria being jealous and angry. He felt it might help him solve his problem. But why was Joan just staring? Was she still angry? Did Gloria's behavior make things even worse for them?

Some lawyer I'll make, he thought as he turned and slunk out of the store. I can't even make my own case against an insane woman with a nutty father.

Joan watched him go. She wondered what in the world had happened. One thing was for sure, though. If there ever had been any kind of liaison between Dick and Gloria, it wasn't going very well now. The thought of saying that to Annie made her smile, but then she felt mean and stopped.

I wonder why he just left though, without even saying hello, she thought. Of course, I was about as wild as Gloria was just now the last time I saw him. I wouldn't be surprised if he were rethinking women in general! Well, I'm not going to let it get me down.

In fact, the little vignette gave Joan a boost, feeling that she had taken the right path in her life. She carried the bolt to the cutting table and watched as the salesgirl unrolled its lovely color. This will be a blouse he'll see me in and wish I were his, she thought.

It was getting dark outside, and not wanting to be out in the cold too long, Joan grabbed her purchase and hurriedly headed for home.

Just as she got to the corner of Laureen's street, she spotted her friend taking out the trash. "Hello Laureen!" she called, waving.

"Hi Joan!" Laureen answered. "Get inside before you catch a cold! By the way, how's Dick feeling? Is he better?"

"Oh, Dick? Yes, he's. . . better." Instantly Joan regretted her response. She felt flagrantly dishonest. But it had been almost a reflex action. Someone asking about Dick seemed natural after the year they'd had, even if most of the time they had been apart.

But Laureen was her friend, and the very person who had introduced Joan and Dick. She felt as if she'd let her down. Laureen had already gone back into her house, so Joan continued home.

At home, Annie was in the kitchen at work at the stove.

"Hi Joan," she called. "Surviving?"

"Yes, thanks," said Joan. "What are you making?"

"You won't believe it, but I'm making you and me a pot of spaghetti sauce."

"Ooooh!" said Joan, forgetting her troubles. "That sounds wonderful!"

"I just have to boil up the macaroni. I stayed home today and I figured we've got that little bit of ground beef, why not? The garlic makes it."

"Oh it sure does!" Joan loved Italian food. And the scent was filling the house in a warm and wonderful way. "What can I do?" she asked grabbing her apron.

"Just set the table. Don't put the plates on, though. We'll use the bowls and I'll serve it from here at the stove."

"What a treat!"

"Bernice'll be over. She said she's bringing a chicken, but it'll keep."

"When she sees this, she won't mind!"

"What's it like out there? I don't think I set foot outside the house the whole day long."

"Windy, and still cold!" Joan ran a glass of water from the spigot. "It always makes me thirsty when it's windy."

"Dries you out."

"Yeah. So," she began, trying to figure out how to tell her story as a report versus gossip.

"What?" Annie was immediately tuned in. She knew that look on Joan's face. There was something new to tell and she hoped with all her heart that it was a positive story. Her friend had struggled to be strong now for over 48 hours. She just might make it through if she stayed strong.

"I went to Kresge's."

"I noticed. What's in the bag?"

"Beautiful fabric," she said smiling. "You have to see it!"

Annie put down her spoon and got the bag from the living room and looked inside. Her eyes gleamed. "Oh, it is beautiful!" She held it up and instantly Joan knew what she would be doing with that fabric. It was pretty on her, but it was perfect for Annie. She smiled and said nothing. But since she and Annie were the same size, making the blouse for Annie would be like falling off a log.

"I like it, too," was all she said, her eyes shining.

"That's funny. When you came in here, I thought you had some news or something, the way you looked. What are you going to make with the fabric?"

"A blouse," Joan said ambiguously.

"That'll make a gorgeous blouse!" Annie said, returning to the pot on the stove.

"Yep," said Joan.

The door opened and Bernice came in with her promised chicken and a few other things. "I'm sorry I'm so late," she said, "but I think I'm glad I'm so late, too!"

Joan laughed. "I knew you'd say that! Nice surprise huh?"

"It sure is!" Bernice looked into the pot and sniffed. "Wow."

"What'd you bring?" Annie asked. "Is there a chicken in there?"

"A chicken, and some chicken livers too, the carrots I told you about, and milk and cream. I also brought, are you ready? A pound of coffee!"

"Oh!" said Annie. "My hero!"

"That's heroine," said Bernice.

"Oh, well, that doesn't flow as well."

"So what were you guys talking about before I came in?"

"Joanie's fabric," said Annie. "Take a look. She's making a blouse."

"That's pretty," said Bernice. "Of course as you know, I've given up the notion of ever sewing."

"Cute," said Annie, "the notion of sewing?"

Joan laughed.

"What?" said Bernice.

"Notion?" said Annie.

"Yeah?"

"Oh never mind."

"I have a story for you guys, but you won't believe it, considering I'm not bursting at the seams with it," Joan said.

Annie's eyes lit up as she turned to look at her. "I knew it!" she said. "Okay, go on."

As Joan filled them in on Gloria's blast-off at the dime store, the girls listened with full attention.

"That's even better than a spaghetti dinner!" Bernice said at the end.

"Okay, then none for you," Annie said.

"Almost better," Bernice corrected.

"But I'm confused," Annie said. "What was Dick doing there? What was Dick doing here in town?"

"You know," Joan said, "that was making me wonder, too. And then, on my way home, I caught sight of Laureen taking out her trash. She yells over, How's Dick feeling? Is he better? And I thought, what does she mean by that?"

"What did you tell her?"

"I said yeah, he was better."

Annie snickered.

"I know. I felt bad as soon as I said it, but I was kind of taken by surprise."

"Well, I would say maybe he and Bob are staying with Laureen, but if they were, how would she not know how he's feeling? Why would she be asking you?"

"What I want to know is was he sick or did he get injured or what?" Joan said. "I didn't notice his being hurt today. He seemed to walk out of Kresge's just fine. So I guess I gave the right answer."

Bernice and Annie nodded. Things were getting very strange. What in the world was going on?

Chapter Sixteen

The atmosphere at the base where Sly and Bobby worked was tense. That morning, the report had come down to all of the employees that another attack had happened during the night. A guard had been injured in a hand-to-hand type attack.

Bobby knew the fellow slightly and was able to talk to him in the infirmary. "Artie, this is my buddy, Sly," Bobby said. "Him and me, we go way back, you can trust him."

"Nice to meet you," Artie said, sitting up in his cot.

"Thanks for warding off that guy," Sly said, offering his hand. "You never know what he'd a done if he'd made it inside."

"You kiddin'?" Artie said. "That's my pleasure, buddy." He was a large, muscular man who did not seem likely to take stuff from anyone. "Guy really ticked me off, sneaking up on me like that."

"Then you were able to see him, describe him?" Bobby asked.

"Hell yeah, I saw him. I told the other MPs, too. They said to me that it would be a help in case he was wandering around in the civilian area."

"What'd he look like?" Bobby said. "We might as well know, too."

"Sure. He's tall, 'bout my height, not as built up. Dark hair really short, and ruddy skin with a funny tattoo on the right hand. That's the one he got me with."

"What did the tattoo look like?" Sly asked.

"Kinda like a cross with points," Artie answered. "Funny looking."

Sly grabbed a piece of paper and sketched a cross that he'd seen many times on papers that the Italians carried. "Did it look like this?" he asked.

"Yeah, that's it. How'd you know?"

"It's Luftwaffe," Sly said. "German Air Force."

"Germans! Here?" said Artie.

"He's probably a hundred miles from here by now or worse. You and I know how easy it is to get a blackout flight to get you out of a jam," he said looking at Bobby. "But at least the MPs know what they're looking for."

"He could be," Bobby answered, "but remember, we were in Europe, the borders aren't so close here, and I don't know how they coulda landed an aircraft anywhere around here without being spotted. There's bases everywhere. Especially after that Sandy Hook catastrophe."

"Well, if they catch'em, we'll know it's him for sure," Artie said, lying back down.

"You could identify him?" Bobby asked.

"Hell yeah—I marked him!"

"What'd you do? Scratch him or something?"

"No, man, I bit him. Right on the neck!"

Sly made a face and Bobby smiled back.

"Well, make sure you get a distemper shot," he chuckled. "Great stuff, man."

Outside the infirmary, Sly shook his head. "That's one tough soldier," he said.

"Oh yeah," said Bobby. "Artie was a Marine. He got a knife wound. Before he got cut, I heard he smacked the guy down with one punch and was getting ready to knock him out with the other. But even after he got that knife to the gut, he had the presence of mind—and the nerve—to take a piece of the guy's neck."

"Jeeze. You wanna get lunch?"

"Made you hungry, did it?" Bobby laughed.

After work, walking the prescribed path, Sly and Bobby discussed the situation at the base. "It's like we're waiting here, sittin' ducks," Bobby said.

"Yeah, cat and mouse kind of thing. I sure don't like the way that feels."

"Me neither. I'd rather be out there on the team looking for this guy."

"Don't tell me you speak German, too?"

Bobby laughed. "No, but I know a few words. The main thing is I want to be doing something on that side. I feel like a pansy sitting here with them guys to protect us."

Sly nodded. "I know what you mean. When this job is over. . ."

"Yeah, when this job is over, what?" Bobby asked.

"I might want to be in that business."

"Sign back on with the military? Annie'd kill ya!"

"No, no, not the military. Maybe the police, you know, detectives."

"Oh detectives! Yeah, I always wanted to be a detective. Workin' on cases like them guys in the movies."

"It's probably not as exciting as that, but I like the idea of trying to figure stuff out, help people out of a jam, that kind of thing."

"I know what you mean," Bobby said, looking off and thinking. "I wonder how many cops they'll need once everybody's back home from this thing."

"Could be a lot more. More people, more cops."

"Yeah."

They walked a while in silence through the open area to their barracks. Then Bobby said, "You tell Annie what you're up to yet?"

"Nah. I want to but I just can't seem to put it together in a letter. We've been writing and it's nice. She seems really—"

Just then they heard shots. Instinctively they got down and took cover under the branches of a nearby tree. After a few moments, they could hear moaning of an MP nearby. With just one hand signal between the two of them, they coordinated the retrieval of the man who had been hit.

Sly had his sidearm out and was scanning the woods around them, looking for any motion or flashes of metal. It was eerily quiet and still. But as soon as Bobby made his move, Sly sent up a volley of fire into the air to distract the shooter and give Bobby a chance to complete his objective.

Bobby was lightening quick, shot out from behind the trunk of the tree, and was on his way back, retrieving the injured soldier who could not walk, by pulling his collar and belt across the ten feet over the rough surface to safety. He situated the man behind the tree with him and Sly and checked over his body while Sly kept watch on the woods where the sniper had gone. The MP had been wounded severely, shot in the hip.

"Looks like a 45 or thereabouts," Bobby said taking off his jacket and wrapping it tightly around the MP. He raised the man's head as best he could without moving him too much, and began to apply pressure on the bullet hole. "I gotta get this bleeding stopped. I'll do that, you keep covering us."

"You got it, buddy," Sly said, who had not stopped scanning the woods for a second. Just then he saw the slightest flicker of a leaf, followed by a second flicker further to the right. His experience in the French woods the previous year had left him an expert in spotting movement, and he stayed on it like a bloodhound on the trail of a rabbit.

As the motion began to follow a pattern, Sly could begin to make out the shape of a man crouched. He wore no helmet but it seemed from his outline that he was carrying a large handgun, just as Sly had guessed. The man sidled toward a thicker part of the wood. Being unfamiliar with the area, he must have thought he was going deeper into the forest.

If he keeps going, Sly thought, I can force him into the barbed wire fence back there and then we can just collect him. As the shooter unknowingly moved even further into the enclosed area, Sly followed with his eyes and made a map of the perimeter of the barbed wire on the ground with a stick. The shooter seemed to be going into the best possible spot for capture. Sly's eyes gleamed with anticipation. His heart pounded as he continued to follow the outline of the man into the trap.

Just as he was about to slink around and follow so that the sniper didn't escape or hide, a shot rang out from the base and the sniper took off running. Sly could see him for only a few more seconds and then he was gone. He felt like strangling the person responsible for ruining the catch. He turned to see another MP, who was running toward them.

"Who'd he get? Aw shucks, Luigi. You still with us, Luigi?" he said puffing from the excitement.

"He's all right," Bobby said, "but he needs a doctor quick. Go and get someone to help us get him in to the infirmary."

"No need, I can carry him in," the soldier said and immediately began to lift the wounded Luigi.

"Let them know Sylvester and Bobby are tracking the shooter," Bobby said. "That's important. I don't think it'll take long to catch him. Just tell your sergeant to send out a couple of MPs and we can show them where the guy went."

After the MP bravely carried his comrade inside, Sly said to Bobby, "You aint no lieutenant anymore, you know."

"I know it," Bobby said, "but I think the kid needed some direction."

"Kid?" Sly said, not taking his eyes from the wood.

"I might be only 5 or 6 years older than him, but it's a big 5 or 6 years," Bobby said.

"I know it," said Sly. "Look between that branch there with the partly broken limb at the end, see it? Down about one-thirty or so?"

"Okay."

"From there, follow it down and maybe four or five degrees to the right, and you'll see—"

"I got it!" Bobby said. "Yeah, he ain't moving."

"No, he's waiting for us to move," Sly said. "Thinks we can't see him and that we're going to give him the chance of a little target practice."

"Soon as the others open that door," Bobby said, "we gotta send him running or he's libel to make mincemeat out of them."

"Ah, you with the food again."

Bobby snickered. "Can't help it."

Just then the door opened again, and the Sergeant and another soldier crept out. Sly was relieved to see that they were not as gun happy as the first one, and he was able to keep his eye on the shooter. "Keep down," he whispered to them, motioning out of sight of the shooter.

Then he sent a volley of shots at the perpetrator and sent him heading straight for the barbed-wire fence.

Bobby motioned the MPs and they advanced, taking cover as they did so. They moved like a team, one advancing and the other leapfrogging beyond him. Once they were into the woods, it was easier to follow the shooter's trail. In only minutes he had run up to the barbed wire fence, turned, and tried to outrun his pursuers.

No more shots were fired, and he was captured, cuffed, and returned to the base detention center by an even bigger soldier than the one who had carried Luigi.

"Those guys were great," Bobby said later, after they'd showered and sat around the common area. "They worked like a pair of pros."

"Yeah. They were pros, I guess," Sly said. "The first guy, the way he came blasting out of there, I had to fire to protect him. But those two that came next, it was like we had it all planned and practiced. They just knew what to do."

"They're probably saying that about us," Bobby said.

Sly laughed. "You know, I know we gotta work out the time on this contract, and hopefully the Army will complete the circumference of that barbed wire fence out there so we survive long enough to make that happen, but I'm thinking about what we were talking about before."

"What, you talkin' 'bout being detectives?"

"Yeah. I think it's kind of the best of both worlds."

"I thought you were an engineer."

"I think my degree, once I finish it out, will be really helpful, you know, trying to figure out criminal pursuits, bombs, abductions, a lot of stuff."

"Hey, yeah. I never thought of that. And how about our language skills. Jeeze, this part of the country, you know."

"I'm not up for that undercover business," Sly said. "Hits too close to going back in."

"Maybe you're right," said Bobby. "You talkin' private detectives or something on the police force?"

"I don't know. Maybe we better see how things develop, Bobby. It could be either. But the cops, well, if you're a cop you have more behind you. Of course if you're private, you can do what you want, but you have to get the cases. You gotta scare up your own business."

"Well, I think it's a good idea we look into it. We can keep tossing it around," Bobby said. "But right now I'm beat."

"Me too. I think I'll write to Annie. See you tomorrow."

At about that time, Harry was hanging up the phone. He looked up to see Helen staring him down, arms crossed and lips pursed.

"What on earth was that about?" she demanded.

Harry stood up, gathered his wife in his arms and said, "Let's dance."

"Oh no, Harry Ashenbach," Helen said, resisting his embrace. "You're not getting away with not answering my question."

"Oh I'll answer it," said Harry. "But first, I have an irresistible urge to hold my wife."

"I think you mean 'contain' your wife," Helen said, giving in a little.

Harry chuckled. "If you need containing," he said. "Let's make like we're on our honeymoon, what do you say? We'll set up a tent right here in the living room and listen to music all night. We can have a fire, roast marshmallows and sing songs."

"Harry, on our honeymoon, we did not join up with the Girl Scouts," Helen said starting to giggle.

"Oh, no, I guess not," said Harry. "That must have been my other honeymoon"

Helen played along. "Yes, because on my other honeymoon, it was a trip to New York City and the finest dining along 5th Avenue. I think I remember getting some jewelry, too."

"Now you're mixing up the two. You got jewelry from me, but only a dinner from the other fellow."

Harry maneuvered her onto the floor in front of the fireplace and got some pillows from the couch. "Now isn't this nice?" he asked.

"Okay, this must be a really big one," said Helen. "A fire and a dance."

Harry stared at the fire and nodded. "Yep," was all he said for a while.

Helen waited, also staring at the fire.

Finally he said, "Well, they've done it again. I put them into spots where they can excel, and it never fails Helen, never fails, where trouble is, you can find Citro and Bapini."

"They're not hurt are they?" Helen said, alarmed.

"No. They did great. They were improvised backup to some real commandos in getting a sniper, Helen. A sniper. I knew the bases were under a mild siege of folks, some of them even local, trying to disrupt the intelligence gathering. But this guy had a gun and everything. Bobby and Sly rescued the guy he shot, forced the shooter into an area where he couldn't escape, and provided cover for the trained team to go and get him. It went like clockwork."

"Well they did well, and they're safe. That's a good thing, isn't it?" Helen asked.

"Yes, from that perspective. But how long do you think they're going to sit and work on trying to decode foreign communications? Now that they've tasted this type of excitement, and outside of the military? We're in for it now, and the girls are going to be very angry with me."

Helen laughed. "Well, they'd be angry with me maybe, but since I didn't get this privileged information until now, I'm in the clear. You don't have to let them know that you knew they were 'under siege,' which sounds probably worse than it is."

Harry nodded, relieved that Helen had not absorbed the full import of the situation. Sly, as well as Bobby, had literally been in a life and death situation. They reacted as any good soldiers would have. But they were certainly in the sniper's sites during several minutes, as he understood it, and risked their own lives to keep the others safe. There was definitely a fiery streak of adventure in those two, Harry thought.

He cradled his wife in his arms, prayed a silent prayer of thanks for her, and for the safety and futures of his former soldiers.

Down the highway and up one floor, Bob and Dick sat talking over coffee about Dick's latest confrontation.

"You sure don't live a quiet life for such a reserved guy," Bob chuckled. "Did she really come apart, right there in the store? What do you do to these women anyway?"

Dick hadn't gotten to the point where it was funny yet, and he sat angsting over the situation. "I don't know, Bob. I'm mystified by these things. I understand at least, that Gloria, well, she's I guess what they call 'stuck' on me, at least for now. But Joan. What is she going to think now, seeing that big scene? I didn't even know what Gloria was going crazy about until halfway through her rant. It was so embarrassing, being in that store and having her act that way."

"Did you come in together?"

"No, the fact is, I don't know when she came in. I was going to get Mama some yarn. Her birthday's coming up, and I wanted to send her a nice package, since I won't be there and all. So I walked there. It was nice out, you know. Well, soon as I get in there, I had just started to see what they had, and I hear first a kind of cooing sound from behind, and then the girl looks off somewhere, must have seen Joan, and starts in about how can I be such a two-timing louse, and on and on, things I can't even remember."

Bob had begun to laugh.

"Well you can laugh," Dick said getting up to put his cup and saucer in the sink.

"Yeah, course I can 'cause it ain't me!" Bob said, continuing to laugh. "Listen, I can't see how the thing did you any worse, and in fact now, maybe that crazy girl will leave you alone."

"I don't know."

"Well, think about it. She's embarrassed herself twice now; once at her home, and then second time today, in a public store. She's gotta be thinking about it and realizing she's made a fool of herself."

"I don't know," Dick said again. "I thought that the first time she carried on about things, but with this girl, you just never know what she's going to do. And I don't see how it can be good for Joan and me. She's liable to think I'm involved with Gloria."

Bob just shook his head. "I'm seeing Laureen tomorrow," was all he said.

Chapter Seventeen

Bernice and Helen met Annie and Joan next morning on the way to early Mass. Joan did not work that day and they had agreed to have a quick breakfast afterwards before Annie had to open the shop.

It was a calm day as they walked down the street, shielded from the pervasive wind with scarves and hats. In St. Benedict's church, the dozens of special intention candles at the foot of Our Lady's statue were fully lit, as had been the norm for several years by then. Their scent and tiny lights within the darkness of the church brought a feeling of peace to most visitors as soon as they entered.

As the women sidled into the pew together, someone tapped on Helen's shoulder as she reached the inside aisle.

"Hello, Helen!" Laureen whispered.

"Laureen!" Helen whispered back. "Sit with us. You can come with us to the diner after. Okay?"

Laureen smiled and nodded and gave a little wave to the others.

Father Bertrand, their wise and caring priest, and the two altar boys processed in as the organist played, and the friends fell to silent prayer, so familiar to them, each with her own thoughts and wishes. The sisterhood they shared while being at Mass was unmatched in any other situation. The closeness that resulted would grow and last forever, warm and loving, like an understated but strong and binding embrace.

After Mass they scurried down the street to the diner and found a booth big enough for all of them.

"We haven't been together like this in ages!" Laureen said, taking off her coat.

"That's for sure," said Bernice. "Or at least what feels like ages."

"What a lovely coat, Laureen," Helen said, feeling the soft dark fur on the collar.

"Thank you!" Laureen said. "It's fake of course, but Mother thought it was time I had something to hide me from this wind. It was a Christmas gift."

"That shows you how long it's been since we got together!" Annie said. "It sure is pretty, Laureen."

"How's Bob doing?" Joan asked, eager to see if she could work out what Laureen had meant about Dick, without letting on that she had fibbed the night before.

"Bob?" Laureen said smiling. "He's wonderful!"

Everyone laughed.

"How are the plans coming along?" Helen asked.

"Well, Dad has offered to make a down payment on that little cottage around the corner from your place, Helen. It's not on Edison, I think it's called Surrey Street. Anyway, we have to take care of that soon because the owner won't wait. But that is fine with us! I can do some decorating and get it all cleaned up before we move in, which will be wonderful."

"I can't think of a finer wedding gift!" Helen said.

Bernice agreed. "You gotta have a place to put all the junk the rest of us are going to give you."

Annie laughed. "Are you hoping for a June wedding?"

"Yes, if that can be worked out, budgeted, I mean," Laureen answered. "They seem to be keeping those bills down," she said, smiling at Joan. "That's a good thing, huh?"

Joan smiled hollowly. "Yeah," she said.

Laureen laughed. "Well don't worry! I'm sure he'll lighten up when it comes to house money!"

Bernice and Annie looked at each other, confused. Laureen was studying the menu and didn't notice. Helen gave Joan a 'what did she mean by that?' look, but no one said anything until the waitress vaporized beside them.

"Yeah?" she greeted.

"Bacon and eggs," said Bernice.

"I'll have toast, coffee, and well-done bacon," said Annie.

"No eggs?" said Helen.

"We got eggs," said the waitress.

"I was talking to—oh, never mind, I'll have coffee and toast with marmalade," Helen said. "Or have you got honey?"

"Yes. Which one?"

"A little of each, please."

"What do you want?" the waitress fired at Joan.

"Mmm, let me see. I think I'll just have some toast and coffee, like Helen there, with some preserves, if you have it."

Laureen was just deciding. "I'll have scrapple and eggs, well done scrapple, please, and whole wheat toast."

Glasses of water landed on the table in front of each of the girls without a drop spilled, and the waitress was back in the kitchen before the first girl took a sip.

"Well, getting back to the wedding," Helen said, still in a fog about Laureen's remarks before. "Do you have your dress yet?"

"I'm wearing Mother's," she said. "But I haven't decided on bridesmaids dresses yet."

"Do you know your colors yet?" Annie asked.

"Of course she knows her colors," Bernice joked. "What color is this, Laureen?" She held up a red scarf.

Everybody giggled.

"I'm thinking blue and white," Laureen said. "I love soft blue and it will probably look nice on everyone, too."

"Oh that will be pretty!" Joan said, forgetting her quest for information. "Gowns or suits?"

"Definitely gowns," Laureen answered. "But I'm looking for something that's not too pricey."

"I can't wait to see you in your dress," Joan said smiling. "You'll be beautiful!"

"We both will be on our days," Laureen said smiling, squeezing her hand.

As they enjoyed their breakfast, no one thought of Gloria, not even Joan. It was a time of purely happy anticipation and the joys of shared friendships.

Walking home, Joan said, "Wasn't it cute the way Bob tapped on the diner window as he walked by on his way to the grocery store? They sure are happy together."

"Yeah, that was," Bernice said. "I'm glad they're having this time because the leg wound and his reaction to it last year made me really worry that they would ever make it to the altar."

Bob McGarrett's leg wound in combat had been so severe that he almost had lost the leg. But the skilled surgeons in the veterans hospital had managed to attach it in such a way that allowed the remaining tissue to knit and eventually form permanent and healthy bonding. But it hadn't been the leg wound that threatened their union. It was Bob's reaction to it, and his belief that he had abandoned his buddy at a time when Dick was in dire need of good medicine.

Both men had looked too closely into the eyes of death to suit them, and ironically, they feared it only for each other. Their brotherhood and strength of character along with many hours of prayer and deep meditation had pulled them through.

"They've sure been through their share of it," Helen said. "All of us have, huh?"

They walked on for a while, and then Helen asked suddenly, "By the way, what did she mean when she said 'they're keeping the bills down,' or something like that? Who is 'they'?"

Annie and Bernice looked at each other again.

"I got no idea," Annie said.

"Maybe she's marrying two guys," Bernice said.

"Funny," said Joan. "Helen, when I came in last night, after Gloria's blow up—"

"Gloria's blow up? Why didn't I hear about that?" Helen said chuckling.

"Oh, believe me, we'll fill you in," Annie said.

"I happened to see Laureen taking out the trash and she said to me, 'How's Dick? Is he feeling better?' Well, I didn't know he was even sick, but when I saw him at Kresge's—

"What?" Helen interrupted again. "How come I don't know about these things!" Then she was suddenly quiet.

"What happened to you, Helen?" Annie asked, her brown eyes laughing just as hard as she was.

It had come to Helen that while she didn't know about the previous day's experiences, she had some secrets herself that needed to be told. And she wasn't sure even still if it was up to her to do the telling. "No, no, I'm sorry, Joan, go on with your story."

"Well, that's all. I told her fine, because I'm a little liar," Joan said. "But—"

"Well you'd better go to confession," Bernice said with mock severity.

"Oh believe me, I know that," Joan said. "But I was trying to get some clues this morning without admitting that I didn't know what I was talking about last night. And as you saw, I didn't get too far."

"Yeah, Helen, you kept asking her about the wedding."

"Oh, I'm sorry Bernice," Helen said, "but if I'd known we were on sleuthing duty, I would have worked it a little differently."

"Well, what we need is some good detective work," Annie said. "Or, alternatively, a good conversation with Bob."

"I'd like to know when I'm going to hear about Gloria and her fireworks display," Helen said.

"Bob?" said Joan, not paying any attention to Helen.

"What Laureen knows, Bob knows," Annie said wisely.

"Yeah. Okay, Annie, you get the job," Bernice said.

As it turned out, no one got the job. It was only minutes after they all arrived at Helen's house that the phone call came. Laureen was in a panic.

"What do I do, what do I do, what do I do?" she cried as Joan took the receiver.

"I don't know!" Joan said. "What is it Laureen?" Her normally calm and collected friend seemed to be winding up and spinning completely out of control.

"Oh I can hardly talk, I can't believe this. Can you come over?"

"All of us?"

"All of you! Now!"

"We're on the way!"

And so just as they had come to the end of their journey, it was coats, hats, and scarves back on and down the road and around the corner to Laureen's house. They scurried as quickly as they could, moving along like a group of schoolgirls late for class.

Laureen greeted them at the door. "Oh Mother, make some hot chocolate. They're here!"

"Hello girls!" cried her mother from the kitchen. "Come on in and warm up by the fire."

Laureen's home was very luxurious, it seemed to Joan and Annie. The fireplace with its huge hearth and surrounding thick carpeting under a wide, welcoming sofa was something they yearned for.

But just then, Joan was not thinking in terms of luxuries. "What is it, Laureen," she whispered so her mother wouldn't hear. "You've got us worried half to death! Is Bob all right?"

"Oh, yes, yes, it's nothing like that," Laureen said, motioning for them to sit down. "He knows, and he's trying to rally the troops on his side of things."

"Rally the troops?" Annie said. "Don't tell me he's reenlisting!"

"He might as well be! But no, not at all. They're going to have to jump into action. Oh Annie, I sure hope we can get Sylvester back!"

"What!" Annie said jumping to her feet.

"No, no, sit down, no, just get him back here in time for the wedding."

"Laureen," Joan said calmer now, "you are not making any sense. What has happened? Sit down, catch your breath and tell us about it."

"Good," said Helen. "If you hadn't done that, I was gonna!"

Joan smiled at Helen.

Laureen licked her lips and sat down as calmly as she could, slowly exhaling. Then she smiled at her mother who had just arrived with a tray of hot chocolates and a plate of sweet rolls.

"Oh join us, won't you?" Helen asked.

Her mother sighed, "Oh my! No time for that! I would love to though, Helen. You and I need to catch up. Maybe after all this is over with! You carry on, Laureen dear, and get things done, hear?"

"Yes, Mother."

Laureen handed out the hot chocolates and put the tray of rolls in the center of the coffee table. Bernice's mouth was twitching.

After a moment of silence, Bernice said impatiently, "Well?"

Laureen nodded slowly as if announcing the death of a President, and solemnly said, "We have to move up the wedding."

"Oh for heaven's sakes," Bernice said shaking her head. "We thought someone had died!" She helped herself to a sweet roll and the twitching stopped.

"I'm sorry, but I don't mean a week or a month, I mean to this weekend! Four days away!"

"Why, Laureen?" Joan asked, relieved and uncharacteristically calm. "This chocolate is good."

"Yes, it is," said Annie nodding.

"Four days, girls! What am I going to do?" Laureen insisted.

"Okay, okay," Helen said. "First tell us how this happened, and then we'll get out some paper, pencil, and make a list of what needs to be done, divide it up amongst ourselves, and see that it gets done. Right girls? We're old hands at this."

"Just as long as she don't say 'old maids,'" Annie whispered to Joan.

Joan giggled.

"My cousin found a resort," Laureen began. "Not just a vacation, but a beautiful, mountain chalet vacation in the Pennsylvania mountains. It has skiing and bonfires and sleigh rides in winter. It's just magnificent. They got together with Mother and Dad and found out what we wanted for our honeymoon and arranged to buy it. They knew we wanted a June wedding, but since it was a surprise and since the only date available was May first, they booked it and so Mother was quietly working on the details of a May first wedding. Bob and I had no idea. I did the choosing of flowers and things, but she was moving things along."

"So what's the problem?" Bernice asked.

"I haven't gotten to that part yet," Laureen said. "This morning, my cousin calls Mother and says, gosh, I just got that check in in the nick of time. I thought it said May, but it actually says Mar, their abbreviation for March! She just said it casually like, oh, by the way, your wedding is this weekend. I've been out of my mind ever since I found out!"

"What a great gift!" Annie said.

"Yeah," Joan said. "Does Bob like the idea?"

"He loves it, but you girls are missing the point!"

"No, no, we're right here with you," Helen said. "We can do this, don't worry. Right girls?"

"Absolutely," said Joan. "Here, have my notebook and pencil, Helen, you have the prettiest penmanship."

"All right, let's start with the hall," Helen said, "and we have food & drinks, music, and for the church, flowers, music, and gowns. We'll need to change invitations to telephone calls where possible, and those far away should be moved to the beginning of the list. We'll use our two telephones and divide the list, right girls?"

Joan and Annie nodded. "What about the food?"

"I can provide what we need to work with," Bernice said, "but I don't think you want me cooking."

Everyone laughed, except Laureen who sat there momentarily stunned.

"How many were you thinking of inviting, dear?" Helen asked.

"Seventy-five," said Laureen hesitantly.

"All right, that's not so bad, is it?"

The afternoon continued and turned into evening. Annie never did open the shop that day, and Bernice never visited the grocery in person, but she did put in a large order for chicken, bread, fruits, flour, sugar, butter, and other necessities for the very rapidly approaching nuptials.

Annie sat at the phone, gleefully dialing the number Helen had gotten from Harry for the hallway phone at the barracks. "This'll be a surprise," she said to Joan who was forming pie crusts in the kitchen. "Hello? Yes, I'm looking for Lt., I mean Sylvester Bapini. Is he by chance around?"

She waited a while and then, "Aha! I caught up with you! Yes, it's me. How are you, darling? Yes. Yes." She giggled. "I'm not just calling to talk, and we only have about 1 minute 25 seconds left of our 3 minutes, so listen, honey. Laureen and Bob are getting married Saturday. You and Bobby and Debbie, whom we'd all like to meet, are invited. Saturday, two o'clock, hurry up wedding. No, just a date discrepancy." She giggled again. "Yes, okay Soldier. You know I love you. I will. I can't wait. Okay, babe. Hey!" she shouted, making Joan start. "They cut us off!"

"Is he coming?"

"Yes," Annie said smiling, "he's coming. I should have thought of this before. Just tell him somebody's getting married. You know, the food and all. Actually this is the first weekend he or Bobby would have been free to leave. They had some kind of training, apparently."

Joan giggled. "It will be great, Annie. You'll see. Everything will be wonderful."

"And for you, too. Dick was on that list, too. I didn't get his name though. Laureen's calling or she said she'd 'tell' him. I think she knows where he is."

"Well of course she knows. But where? And who's 'they'? That's what I want to know," Joan said, rolling out another crust. "I think we'll get four pie crusts out of this ball. How many pies again?"

"Seven. Well 'they' is not Gloria if that's what you're worried about. He's certainly not staying at her house."

"She sure has room in that mansion. But no, you're right. If he ever was, he certainly isn't now."

"Bob? You think Bob? Maybe that's what she meant, but Bob was at her house, wasn't he Joanie?"

"They both were, yes." Joan sighed. "You know what? He's coming, that's good enough for me. If we're still engaged, we'll work it out. But for now, we've got to go through the night with these pies and the gowns."

Helen and Bernice made phone calls at Helen's house while Harry visited a friend about getting chairs for the church hall. The dinner would be in the church right after the ceremony and photos would be taken by Father Bertrand, who would also perform the ceremony. Monsignor Kuchesky was visiting friends in

Baltimore, but he had written a special prayer for the couple, to be read at the offertory.

"I hate to make you call all of the strangers," Helen said. "I could take some of them."

"That is all right," said Bernice.

Helen chuckled. "You said that just like Margaret!" said Helen.

"I think I did, didn't I? We will need to get in touch with her, too, and her Elwood."

"Definitely. She's probably on our list as well."

"I'm not excited about the pattern party for tomorrow," Bernice said. "I always look so awful in formal wear."

"Not the way Joan sews you won't," said Helen. "She's getting to be a real pro. I think she fits clothing better than you can buy it made up. But Laureen's going to have to come through with the rest of that fabric very soon!"

When Harry returned home, announcing that he had arranged for the chairs, tables, utensils and warming trays, Helen gave him a big hug. "You are a prize," she said. Then quietly aside, "You dodged a bullet. Maybe neither of us will have to fess up to knowing about Sylvester's cops & robbers games, but you will drive up there and pick them up, right?"

"Yes, I will, Mrs. Ashenbach," Harry said.

Chapter Eighteen

"I think it's okay about the party," Annie said, as she peeled potatoes at the sink.

"What party?" Joan asked.

"The one we're not having," Annie said. "You know how they do a pre-wedding day party."

"Oh, you mean the bachelor party? We wouldn't be involved in that!"

"No, I mean the one for the bride."

"I didn't know there was such a thing."

"Well, there is in It'ly," Annie said. "Least I think there is. It's for the bride. It's real nice. But it's okay that they're not doing that."

"I think they have enough to do without another party. Pulling this one off is going to be heroic!"

"Yep, that is for sure. How many of these I gotta peel?"

"I think it's a hundred," Joan said, paging through the binder for the directions. "We figured on 75 people, and each one eating an average of one and a third potatoes."

"You never know about things like this," Annie said, dumping a pile of peelings into the paper bag that lined the kitchen trashcan. "What if somebody comes along and dumps half of a big serving bin onto his plate? Then you're stuck with not enough to feed the rest of the people."

"It always seems to work out. If you're worried about that, sometimes people have a server go around with a scooper and plop a scoop of potatoes on each person's plate, unless they don't want any."

"That sounds like the school cafeteria."

Annie laughed. "Without the food fight!"

"I'll get a knife and help you out in a minute," Joan said, "I just want to check off what we've done and what we've got left to do."

"You can check off the dresses. Gosh, Joanie, the dresses are beautiful. You really are gifted."

"Oh you can sew, too!" Joan said. "I appreciate it, but you're no beginner yourself."

"You think you might want to learn how to design clothes some day?"

"Oh, I don't know about that. Maybe though. Every now and then if I haven't been able to do any sewing for a while, I just get all fired up and in the mood to make something!"

"Creativity yeah. That really is important to us, you know?"

"It's sure gotten us through a rough couple of times, hasn't it?"

"Yes," Annie said, remembering how many dances and food tables the four of them had set up and cooked for over the past few years. "Hey, you think Laureen will be cooking and sewing for our weddings?"

"I know I'll be doing those things for yours, for sure!"

"And me for you," Annie said.

"If we're not old maids," Joan said. And then started to giggle.

"Yeah, you better laugh," Annie said scowling and shaking her head.

"When does Sly get here?"

"I'm not sure. Have you heard if Dick is coming?" Annie asked, holding the name 'Dick' with a long 5-second pause.

"You know Annie, I think it's time for me to own up to my meanness and admit that the argument was my fault."

"Well it's about time!" Annie said.

Joan dropped her pen and looked up, astonished. "You mean you thought that all along?" she asked.

"No, but it's been quite a while since he came here looking to take you to lunch. And really, Joanie, I'm your best friend, but I gotta tell you, that man did nothing wrong."

Joan looked at the floor. "I know, I know," she said. "It just hit me wrong, and I was so vulnerable. There's no excuse, though. Gloria just . . . gets to me. I guess I feel sorry for her because I'm the lucky one, or was at least. And she's just always wanted him and well, you know. But I am dying to see him, talk to him."

"What will you say to him?"

"I don't know exactly, but I plan to own up for the trouble." She thought about it for a while, and started to giggle mischievously. "And then I'll ask him what on earth happened at Kresge's that day!"

Just then someone tapped on the door and came in.

"It's gotta be Bernice," Annie said.

"Gotta be," Bernice said. "It's me and Helen. Or Helen and I, I guess."

"Hello girls, how are you making out?" Helen called. "Your living room sure tells a story!"

The ordinarily tidy room was covered with dresses, dishes, tablecloths, and even several pairs of shoes. "It's wedding central around here," said Annie.

"At Helen's house, too," Bernice said. "You should see it. Of course I feel like the operator these days."

"How are your calls coming?" Joan asked.

"Well, I finished making the calls, but now we're taking regrets."

"Do you have a count yet?" Annie asked.

"Yeah, she's worried Sylvester's going to come by and take half the mashed potatoes and there won't be enough!" Joan said laughing.

"Maybe not Sylvester, but somebody might," Annie said.

"Well, I can see why she's worried. Remember Christmas dinner?" Bernice said, laughing along. "I thought we were going to have to go back to the kitchen and start cooking all over again in the middle of the meal!"

"He's not that bad," said Annie.

"I like a man to be a good eater," Helen said. "It's always so satisfying."

"You know, one person I haven't been able to get in touch with," Bernice said, "is Margaret. Do you think she'd rather just get the phone call from one of you?"

"Oh I don't think it's anything like that!" Helen said. "How many times have you tried?"

"I guess three, and the first time, someone said she wasn't at home. After that, no one has answered at all. Do you see her at the shop at all, Annie?"

"I haven't been at the shop! I'll tell you, this rush to the altar definitely came at a good time. If it was just before Christmas, I don't know if we could have managed."

The afternoon passed quickly, and by day's end, the lion's share of the food had been taken to the church hall refrigerator, and all of the tables and chairs were in place.

As they wound down the evening, making sure all of the dresses were there, and their matching shoes, Joan and Annie felt good.

"We've never done this for a friend before, have we?" Joan asked.

"No. It's always been for a lot of worthy people, but never like this. I guess it's a good thing we've gotten in the practice from all those dances and dinners. Remember frying up all that chicken last year?" Annie laughed. "I thought we'd never get to the end of that chore. But we did."

"It made a lot of people happy," Joan said, remembering the hungry young men, away from home for the first time in their lives, eagerly grabbing fried chicken from the baskets on the tables. "I think your mother's wedding cake is going to be a smash, and all of those luscious desserts, especially now, Annie. I wish we could eat one of those tarts!"

"I hope there's enough of everything. Helen said Bernice got 68 definites. But you know, she never heard back from Margaret. I haven't heard about any accidents or anything, have you?"

"No," Joan said thoughtfully. "Maybe she's busy making plans of her own, though. I don't know when her date is and it could be coming up soon, too. She was dependent on Elwood's schedule, and you know how the Army is."

"Yeah, do I." Annie smiled. "I cannot wait for tomorrow."

"What time are they supposed to arrive?" Joan knew what Annie meant, and it wasn't that she couldn't wait for the wedding, which was exciting enough.

"You know, Joanie, I almost feel like it's me and Sly's day tomorrow. I was so depressed and so sad when he left, and so confused. And now it's like, everything is fine as long as we see each other. He sounded so good on the phone. I don't know what's changed."

"You've changed," Joan said. "I'm not sure how, but I think you have."

"Yeah, which I guess started when you accused me of having a new best friend."

Joan shook her head. "Oh don't remind me! I can't believe how awful I've been acting."

"Not any worse than me. I am so worried about how I will look to others that I just don't let anyone in, even you. And that's a mistake I think. You're always so open and what's bothering you is always easy to see."

"I don't think Dick would agree with that!" Joan said with a sad smile.

"Well, I think you have changed, too, Joanie. It's not like you wouldn't have helped your dear friend before, but you were 'all in' in this, like it was your own wedding. It's been great working on this with you and Helen and Bernice, but especially you."

Joan smiled. "You know, Annie I do feel changed. If we just keep going on our own paths, the ones we feel are right, it seems like we do grow. Seems like we grow along the way, and for the better if it's the right path, the right choices."

They were quiet for a few minutes, thinking about Laureen's big day and how things would go for them as well.

"Well," Joan said quietly, "one thing is for sure. With me and Dick, I'm going to make sure I say the right things, and just hope I can make him see that whatever becomes of us, I value, I truly love what's between us."

"Good."

"Yep," Joan nodded, drifting off to sleep sitting up, "Tomorrow's the day."

Just outside of town, in the apartment that Bob and Dick called home, and which would soon include Laureen for a few weeks, Bob fussed with the bow tie around his neck.

"I don't think it looks right. It must be the wrong size," he said, tugging at it.

"I don't believe they come in sizes," Dick said as calmly as he could. He had responded to the same remark, at last count, six times. "Why don't you take it off for now and see if it looks better to you in the morning."

"The morning! That would be way too late to replace it."

"Ah, yes." Dick shook his head and sighed. He had heard about bride jitters before a wedding, but he had not known that the grooms were just as vulnerable. There would be no point in mentioning to Bob that the shop where they'd gotten the ties had been closed for hours. Not only was Dick certain that Bob already knew that, mentioning it out loud might get Bob's nerves even more frayed. "Well, just for the record, and I'm a very accomplished tie guy, I say the tie looks just about perfect."

Bob stopped tugging at it and stood still, looking at his reflection. "I think it might be this mirror," he finally said. "It's beveled, you know, and that makes everything look uneven."

"So it does," said Dick, noncommittally.

Bob laid his tuxedo across the couch. "Don't sit there."

"I won't."

"I'm going to change. I need to unwind," Bob said.

"No kidding," said Dick under his breath.

"Huh?"

"Oh nothing. Listen, the time, Bob. When are we expected tomorrow?"

"We gotta get there early. It starts at 2:00, so I guess 1:00.

"A whole hour, okay."

"Yeah, I think that's what she said."

"I'll be going with you, so you'll be on time."

"I'm good with time," Bob said shortly. "I've always been very punctual."

"I know it," said Dick. He wanted to ask Bob if he was feeling nervous, but he didn't want to open a can of worms.

As it turned out, Bob came out with, "Geeze I'm nervous!" He picked up his tux, laid it back down, and picked it up again. "I don't know how to be a husband. What in the world do husbands do, Dick?"

"Well, they—"

"I don't even know if Laureen is ready for all this. We moved the date up, you know. It would have been three months from now, or longer. But we moved it up and I don't know if either of us is ready."

As Dick watched his friend begin pacing and puffing and nearly hyperventilating, it occurred to him that he could just as easily keep his buddy company sitting down. So he did, without sitting on the tux.

"What are you doing sitting down!" Bob said stopping and glaring at him.

"You just answered your own question."

"I mean this is serious. How can you just sit there?"

"Do you want me to go with you to Laureen's?"

"For what!"

"To tell her to call off the wedding. Let her know you're not ready, and that you don't feel she's ready either."

"What are you, crazy?" Bob said, shaking his head, looking at Dick as if he were spinning on his head and breathing fire.

"Bob, look, I'm just trying to—"

"I know, I know, I know. Never mind!" Bob said and stormed off to his room, then came back ten seconds later, grabbed the tuxedo and tried to storm off again, but the hanger got snagged on a fiber from the couch and yanked him down to where he had to unhook it.

Dick struggled, trying not to laugh. He and Bob were brothers to the core, and he would never let him down if there were any possible way he could avoid it, but the show was getting wilder and wilder, and there was no other way to see things than as the pre-wedding comedy of nerves that it was.

Bob heard him holding back a laugh and glared hard at him. "You put this here, didn't you?" he demanded, finally getting the hanger disconnected from the sofa.

"I wouldn't do that," Dick said as solemnly as possible.

"Oh sure!" Bob said and stomped off to his room.

Dick sighed and got himself a glass of milk and some graham crackers. Might be a long night, he told himself. Sustenance may prove useful.

Chapter Nineteen

"Good morning, good morning, good morning!" called Bernice.

"What are you, the greeting committee?" Annie asked drying her hands in the kitchen as Bernice charged through the door.

"Yes, a committee of one," Bernice said. "What are you up to? Still in your pajamas I see."

"Joanie's in the shower. I'm waiting. You're up and out early!"

"I just thought we'd go together," Bernice said.

"That's a good idea. Laureen wants Joanie to go there before the wedding, being that she's her Maid of Honor, so it's you and me."

Bernice nodded, smiling. "I wonder how Laureen's doing today!" she whispered conspiratorially.

"I don't even want to speculate," Annie whispered back. "Joanie's the one who's going to have to help her through the jitters.

"I bet Joan's going to be nervous herself!"

"Joan? What's she got to be nervous about?"

"She has to walk up the aisle before the bride. It's nerve-wrecking, like being on a stage or something," Bernice said, her eyes wide. "Glad it's not me!"

"Oh you'd be great," Annie said. "With all of your singing practice? You wouldn't have a problem in the world."

"No, remember, I sang from the back of the church. I wasn't out in front and nobody was looking at me either. They were listening, but not looking. No, I don't think I'd do well as the object of attention. Of course I don't plan to take that particular journey down the aisle ever myself, anyway."

"You never know," said Annie.

"Oh yes I do know," said Bernice resolutely.

"Okay, okay," said Annie. "But even when you're sworn in as a nun—"

"You don't get sworn in. It's not like you're an elected official, Annie."

"Well whatever they call it, the oath of Sisters or something—"

"Vows," said Bernice, rolling her eyes. "They call it vows. Final vows are binding. But go on."

"Thank you! When you take your final vows, aren't you in front of a lot of people then, too?"

"Well. Gosh, I don't know." Bernice thought for a minute. "I think you do it with a group of other novices. But I'm not sure."

"I don't care how nervous I am, when my day comes, I'm marching straight down that aisle!" Annie said, pouring a cup of coffee. "You want one?"

"Sure." Bernice sat down at the kitchen table. "This is nice. I'll miss this once you're married and off somewhere."

"Yeah," said Annie. "You probably will."

"Well I hope you will too!" Bernice said.

Annie giggled. "You know I will! But I have a feeling we're still going to spend a lot of time together."

"Of course, I'll probably be getting pretty busy if I start this nursing program. Oh, that's right! I got the news this morning. I've been accepted into the hospital training program."

"Great news! Congratulations Bern! How did you manage that?"

"How did I manage it? Thanks a lot! Did you think I'm brainless?"

Annie laughed. "Well, yeah."

"You want a piece a me?" Bernice said, boxing the air.

"Nah," said Annie shaking her head. "You're too small. If I took a piece, there'd be nothing left to talk to."

"Well, that's a nice thing to say!" Joan said, rushing into the kitchen. "Is there any coffee left or did you two drink it all?" She shook the percolator and then set it back down. "Oh good!"

"Yeah we left you some," said Annie. "But I'm not sure you should have any. You already seem a little excited. You think the coffee will do you any good?"

"I need something hot," Joan said. "But gosh girls, I'm nervous! Do I look all right?"

"Well, so far," said Annie.

"What do you mean? You don't like my hair?"

"Your hair looks great," said Bernice, "but you are planning to put on a dress, aren't you?"

"Oh! My dress!" shrieked Joan, slamming the cabinet door. "Why didn't you tell me?" And she ran out of the kitchen whimpering.

"See what I mean?" Bernice said.

"We've got lots of time yet," Annie said. "Maybe we can figure out a way to get her into a calmer state of mind."

"I don't think anything short of a ballpeen hammer is going to do that," Bernice said.

Annie shook her head. "Yeah, but I bet when her day comes, she'll be as cool as a cucumber."

"You don't know Joan too well, do you?"

"I'm just sayin'" Annie said, getting up to put the cups away.

"Hey, listen," Bernice said suddenly serious. "I'm getting a little concerned. Have you seen Margaret at all?"

"Seen her? No, not since, well, I can't remember. Why do you ask? Are you and she still at it? Come on Bernice."

"No, we aren't. Or at least the I part of we aren't, isn't, amn't, or whatever you say. I just can't find her."

Annie stopped short. "Well what are you looking for her for?"

"I'm supposed to invite her to this wedding," Bernice explained. "Nobody's been able to tell me a thing. I even tried calling around to see if anybody had seen or talked to Elwood. It's like they never existed."

"That's really odd," said Annie, thoughtfully.

"It really is. I don't know what to do. Any ideas?"

"I would say let's ask Joanie, but I'm worried it might be the straw that breaks the camel's back."

Bernice nodded. "I don't think she has anyway. I asked her before, and she would have told me if she had. Joan's really good that way."

"Joan's good what way?" Joan asked, standing in the door, properly attired.

"Oh how pretty!" Annie said. "They're going to be looking at you instead of the bride!"

It was true. Joan was such a beauty and in the soft, blue dress Laureen had chosen for her, her blue eyes shown and sparkled. The Maid of Honor was to wear an embedded tierra with her veil and it drew attention to her lush, golden locks.

"They'd better not be!" Joan said, just as nervous as ever. "Joan's good what way?"

"Let's rethink the ballpeen hammer," Annie said under her breath.

"You're good with remembering what people need," Bernice said. "You haven't heard from Margaret, have you? Since I asked you, I mean?"

"Oh. No, I haven't. You still haven't heard from her?"

"No, and nobody answers her phone. I meant to go over to the church to see her there. I put it off because I didn't want to interrupt her for something personal at work. But now it's too late. I'm really getting worried."

"I'm sure she's just been busy," Annie said, trying to soothe the girls. "After all, she's a bride-to-be as well."

"Yeah," said Bernice. "Well, I hope that's all it is."

"Bernice has been accepted into the hospital nursing program, Joanie," Annie said. "When do you start Bernice?"

"I don't think it's until the fall, but I don't have any specific dates yet, only that I was accepted into the next semester."

"Congratulations, Bernice," Joan said, "but I don't have time to talk about that right now. I've got to get going! Good-bye girls!"

She grabbed her coat and rushed out the door. Two seconds later, the door opened and she grabbed her hat from the end table, put it on, checked herself in the mirror, and then looked down to make sure she had her dress on, and rushed out a second time, slamming the door.

"You think Laureen's got one of them hammers?" Annie asked.

Joan walked hurriedly down the sidewalk. Ironically, the closer she got to Laureen's house, the calmer she began to feel. After all, she told herself, Laureen was going to need someone to lean on. It had been a difficult four days. Yes, it was true, she and Annie and Bernice and Helen had worked very intensively to get everything ready for the reception and even did some of the work for the ceremony itself. But Laureen had to rush decisions that any other bride would have had months, sometimes a year or more, to make.

In the end, Joan felt, Laureen had done a wonderful job. Her color choices, the flowers, the gowns, the music, they would combine to make a very lovely and memorable most special event in her life.

Joan took a deep breath and let it out. It was such a special day for Laureen, and her thoughts had been entirely on her friend. But it just then occurred to Joan that today she was very likely to finally see Dick again. The thought gave her a completely different kind of nervous that she was not sure if walking would alleviate.

What if he's angry and won't even talk to me, she thought. What if, oh please God, what it he comes to the wedding with Gloria?

She couldn't bear the thought of it. But she must push those thoughts from her mind, which she did quite well. Her friend needed her and she needed to be there for her.

At Laureen's, for once, there was no fire in the fireplace and the amount of activity seemed impossible for only three people.

Laureen was standing in the living room, her beautiful golden hair coiled softly around her face, with a generous roll falling down in the back, resting on the pure white satin of her mother's perfectly fitted gown. The sight of her made Joan catch her breath.

"Laureen!" she said. "You're stunning!"

Laureen turned, and it was clear she had been crying. "Do you really think so?" she asked. "I can't get my hair to lay right in the front and it's too late to change the style. If I can't get it to lay down, the veil won't look right and the whole dress will be ruined!"

"Oh, no, it's not ruined. Here let me help," Joan said going to her.

"Maybe you can calm her down," her mother called from the kitchen where she sat putting a button on her husband's jacket. "She's been up and down emotionally all morning!"

Joan smiled at Laureen. "You know it's just nerves, don't you? I was nervous myself, thinking about walking ahead of you in the church, but we're both going to be fine."

"But Joan, it's for the rest of my life!" Laureen wailed. "It's so soon! What do I do?"

"What you do is remember," Joan said soothingly, "is remember those awful, painful nights of worrying about Bob, not knowing where he was, if he was safe, if he was even still alive. And think now, from this day forward, I can be with him, love him, be loved by him, and make a life with him."

Laureen's tortured expression had softened when Joan began to talk, and by the time she had finished, her eyes were closed and she was smiling self-consciously. She looked at Joan and shook her head slowly. "You are so right," she said. "Thank you." She squeezed her hand and exhaled slowly. "Help me get this veil on, will you?"

"Are you making any progress in there, Joan?" Laureen's mother called from the kitchen.

"We're fine, Mom," said Laureen. Then, turning to Joan, she said, "My uncle is coming to drive us four to the church, and we'll get there early so we can make sure everything is ready. We'll be leaving in a couple of minutes."

"Oh, so early?"

"Yes, I think an hour is good," Laureen said, turning her face away and smiling. She might have had a little tension herself, but nothing was going to stop her from helping Joan in a way Joan clearly needed the help.

It wasn't long before Laureen's uncle pulled in the driveway, and shortly afterward, they all arrived as planned at the church. Laureen and Joan were guided to a little back room neither of them had ever known existed, where Laureen took off her over coat and began to apply fresh makeup.

"What can I do to help?" Joan said. "It looks like you've got that all under control."

"You know, when we came in, they were asking about the reception in the hall. I don't think they knew where to put the tables and chairs. Can you maybe go there and see if they are still working on that and just tell them how you and the girls have it worked out? That would really help."

"Oh sure," Joan said. "Believe me, I can help in that department!"

"Thanks Joan, you're such a good friend!" Laureen said, giggling silently.

Outside, some of the altar boys who had volunteered to help out moving the tables and chairs, and the two who would serve at the wedding had begun to arrive. Some on bicycles and others on foot. As Joan crossed over to the hall, she saw that there were a couple of cars parked there, but Helen's was not one of them. One looked vaguely familiar.

Inside the hall, Bob was carefully instructing the boys to follow his friend's directions. Just as Joan entered the hall, Bob was leaving to go to the front of the church to meet with Father Bertrand.

"Oh, hello there," he said smiling, almost laughing. "So nice to see you!"

"Don't you look handsome!" Joan said smiling back, thinking gosh, Bob must be nervous too! He's sure full of the funnies this morning.

"Why thank you! I'm a little nervous, but I think I got most of that out of my system yesterday. Are you here to help us figure out this seating thing?"

"Yes," Joan said. "Laureen said, oh and she's beautiful by the way!"

"Oh, don't torture me!" Bob said, clutching at his heart dramatically.

Joan laughed. "I'm happy to help but it's pretty simple."

"Would you mind telling the guys? I've got to run and see Father before it gets too late."

"Oh of course," said Joan. "Go ahead. Where are they?"

"He's just inside," Bob said mysteriously. And he left, openly laughing.

Well what is so daggone funny, Joan wondered. She shook her head and shut the door after him to keep out the cold, and went in to find the young men moving chairs. But what she found was one extremely handsome man in a tuxedo, who had just heard the entire exchange between Joan and Bob and was waiting to see her come in.

"Hello, Joan," Dick said, his eyes filled with a pain and anticipation Joan found herself instantly wanting to vanquish.

"Dick! Oh, so you're—oh. Hello."

"You look beautiful," he said. "The blue gown, your hair, everything."

"Thank you." Joan smiled faintly. "You'll have to give me a minute to catch my breath."

Dick smiled. "Well that sounds hopeful."

"Hopeful?"

His face fell again.

"Dick," said Joan, moving closer to him, "let's sit down and talk for a minute. Okay?"

"Yes. I would like that."

"I wanted to talk to you earlier, but I didn't have your mother's telephone number or even your address there. And I could have gotten it from Bob, but ever since the wedding had to be moved up, well we've just been nonstop activity, and—"

"My mother's address?" Dick said confused. "What did you want to say to her?"

Joan laughed nervously. "Well, nothing. I wanted to talk to you."

"Oh," said Dick. "Well you didn't know then." The idea seemed to make him lighten up a little.

"Know what?"

"I live with Bob."

"At Laureen's? Oh! Of course he's not there now. Well, where does Bob live?"

"Just a bus ride down from town. Nice little apartment."

"Oh," said Joan. "Okay. Well, I'll say it now. I just want you to know that even though I know you've been seeing Gloria, and maybe our chance has gone, I will always have deep feelings of love and respect—" her voice caught as she fought back the tears.

"Wait," Dick said. "Seeing Gloria?"

"Yes."

"No." He shook his head. "Gloria? Why would I see Gloria? I don't care for Gloria." He almost laughed thinking of the incident at Gloria's house. "But she does."

Joan didn't get what he had said at first, but when she did after a moment, it brought a smile. "I didn't hear from you and Bernice saw you going to her house and then Gloria told us at the diner that you were seeing her and—"

"And then you saw that bizarre scene in the dime store."

"Yes! And that seemed to confirm it, you know, a lover's quarrel."

"Joan, I would have called, but what you said that day—"

"I know it, I know it. I'm so ashamed. And I'm so sorry I didn't even let you speak. Then Laureen asked me if you were better, so I knew you'd gotten sick that day, and I just felt terrible! And now, I don't know what you must think of me, but please believe me, it's all the emotion, all my deep feelings so bottled up waiting to see you, be with you—it left me so vulnerable and I said those terrible things to you. I just hope you can forgive me. I can't blame you if your feelings have totally changed."

"Nothing's changed, for me, Joan but—"

"Not for me either!" Joan declared sincerely, wanting so badly to be in his arms.

"But I can't marry you—"

"Oh!" Joan felt the air sucked out of her lungs.

"for three years," Dick finished.

"Oh." The air came back. "Three years. Why three years?"

"Because I have finally recognized my calling and how I'm to be able to serve it. It's been a long time coming, but I want to go to law school, Joan. The government will pay, but I won't be earning a very good living, and I just can't support a wife and myself until I get the degree and begin working."

Joan was struggling in the midst of a wild assortment of emotions, but she had one greatest desire among them and that was to feel his arms around her.

They might well have been of one mind, as Dick stepped ever closer and pulled her into a loving, life-restoring embrace. They might never have let go of each other had it not been for a tug on Dick's sleeve.

"Mister," said the altar boy, "is this right?" The little fellow indicated the arrangement of the chairs and tables.

Dick looked at Joan, eyebrows raised.

"Yes," Joan said smiling brilliantly. "This is perfect."

Chapter Twenty

The regal chords of the Pachelbel Cannon washed through St. Benedict's as Bernice, Annie, Helen, and finally Joan slowly processed up the aisle to their places in the front pews. The gentle blue gowns flowed gracefully as they joyfully preceded their dear friend, as they supported her in this most holy and precious ceremonial of her life.

Helen spotted Harry across the aisle sitting with the men and caught his eye. He winked at her, and raised his eyebrows and nodded. She smiled back. Sometimes he made her feel like a young girl just getting to know him.

Annie nodded to Sylvester, who along with Bobby, had only just arrived before the ceremony, but in enough time to run like a lion to give Annie a hug and a kiss, right there in front of everyone, as Bobby tugged at his arm, saying "Come on, now, they're waitin' for us, aww Sly. Come on!" The bride's party giggled, and Sly and Bobby nearly ran down the side aisle to get in his spot in the pew, while Annie readjusted her veil and Joan fixed her sleeves. As Sly's eyes followed her up the aisle, he wondered how she would feel about his decision to protect and serve.

As Bernice inhaled the rich scent of the incense and her heart pounded to the glory of the sacred music, she longed for the time when she would take these steps again, to place her life into the hands of Christ in total service to Him. The music was intoxicating. Her plan to create a small but ambitious choir was utterly decided by the experience of that day.

Joan's heart had never been so full as she proceeded steadily up the aisle toward Dick. She was shy to look at him, but her wish just to see him was stronger, and their eyes locked in love as she took her place beside where Laureen would stand.

And finally, the Cannon was over and the bride's entrance began. Laureen was glorious in her shimmering white gown, pearl buttons and long tapered sleeves. Her golden hair looked like a halo, while her joyful tears sparkled like diamonds. The admiration in her father's eyes, and the pride he felt were contagious and brought a new wave of warmth and joy to the whole congregation. Laureen took her place, accepted her father's kiss with grace, and squeezed Joan's hand as Father Bertrand began the ceremony.

Life would change that day for Laureen and Bob, Joan thought, and while they were the lucky couple that day, they were also the brave couple, taking the challenges into a new way of life. Joan couldn't help wondering how things would be for them, having had to rush the ceremony in order to keep their honeymoon. The irony of it made her smile.

As the Mass progressed to Holy Communion, Annie noticed for the first time, that statues of angels were now stationed at either side of the altar on marble shelves. They seemed to be watching below, guarding the souls who partook of the sacraments, keeping them safe. Annie smiled and bowed her head in a separate prayer of thanks for the guidance and love of the angels. Just then she felt a profound desire to help do their work, to help keep others safe. She looked up to see Sly looking thoughtfully at her. Peacefully, she smiled at him.

At the first kiss between Bob and Laureen as man and wife, the ceremony blended with the celebration as joy and happiness followed for hours.

Helen stood at a command post in the hall's kitchen, coordinating the heating of the foods, while the young boys helping took orders on which things to take from the refrigerator and where to put them. By the time the photos had been taken, and the wedding party and guests were seated, Helen had all the hot foods ready, the rolls and butter distributed to the twelve tables, and fruit salads on trays that Annie, Joan, and Bernice were quickly taking around. Once the cold foods were served, the girls returned for large serving bowls of chicken and mashed potatoes, gravy and vegetable casseroles for each table.

"I won't make it a long blessing," Father began smiling, "because I can see that everyone, including our young helpers, are very much ready to have supper! But I just want to offer our thanks to God for a beautiful wedding ceremony and celebration, and prayers that this holy union will be blessed with great happiness throughout the years."

Laureen and Bob, who sat as close as their chairs would allow, smiled.

"Amen to that!" called Bobby.

"Shh," said Debbie. "You can always tell where the guys from South Philly are sitting," she said quietly.

But everybody laughed and dinner began.

"Hey, you got a dinner date, there tall beauty?" Sly said as Annie came to take her seat at the wedding party's table. "I wasn't sure if you were going to eat or just run around with dishes all night."

"You're the one who's with the dish," Bobby said.

"Well, we had to do our duty first," Annie said, "but it's all downhill from here. And thanks," she said to Bobby. "I think I like your friend," she said turning to Sly.

"This is great chicken," Bobby said. "You make this stuff, Annie?"

"Nope, you'll have to thank Helen and Joan for that," Annie said. "But if you like the mashed potatoes or casserole, you can tell me."

"Hey, I like it all!" Bobby said.

"Who didn't know that?" Sly answered.

Joan giggled, as she found her space next to Dick and sat. Her heart was pounding again just to be close to him. He put his arm around her as soon as she sat and gave her a kiss on the cheek.

"I've been dying to do that since this afternoon," he whispered in her ear, giving her a chill.

She smiled and looked around to see if anyone was watching. Everyone was watching.

Bernice started to giggle, then Annie, and Helen, who had just finished up in the kitchen appeared, and laughed, too, not knowing what it was all about, but happy to be getting off her feet.

"You just missed Master Sgt. Thimble's sneak attack," Harry told her, and everyone laughed again.

"Well it's about time," Helen said to no one in particular.

"Yes, I have a feeling," Dick said smiling shyly, "that Bob and Laureen, who ordered us both to help out with a job that was already done, might have something to do with it. And I just want to say—"

"Yes?" said Bob.

"Yes?" echoed Laureen, giggling and poking her head into view from the other side of Bob.

"Thank you," said Dick.

"It's the least we could do," Bob said. "This guy saved me from strangling myself with my bowtie last night. A toast to Dick Thimble!"

"Make it to Joan and Dick, and I'll drink to that!" Dick said.

"All right, to Joan and Dick!"

"Here, here!"

After dinner, as Annie and Sly sat talking amongst themselves, Sly decided the time was right to drop the bomb. "Annie," he began, "I been lying to you."

"You're really a woman?"

"Be serious," he said. "My job? It's a little higher risk than I led you to believe. In fact, there's been some shootings and a couple of guys have gotten hurt."

"Sly! What on earth are you doing?"

"It's not so much what we're doing, it's the fact that what we're doing makes us targets to these international guys who don't want us finding out stuff. The attacks on the two guards that got shot were by foreign nationals. We're on the base, and we're protected, but to be honest, anything can happen."

"And I have a confession for you," Annie said.

"Uh oh!" said Bobby.

Sly looked suddenly tense.

Joan stifled a laugh. "She's been seeing Gloria."

Everybody laughed.

"Everybody might as well hear it," said Annie, "because I'm never going to do it again. But one time when you and Bobby were in Helen's kitchen, you didn't know I heard, but you were talking about this job, the spy stuff, and code and so forth. I was ashamed that I stood there listening, and it really did a number on me before you came clean about it."

"Oh Annie! Bobby told me to tell you right away—"

"Yeah I did," Bobby joined in, his mouth full of bread.

"But I didn't think you'd like it, but the job was— hey, let's walk over here for a couple minutes' privacy."

They stepped away from the table.

Annie was insistent. "Well why don't you do something else, Honey? Something closer. There's plenty of work around here, and there's going to be more as time goes on."

"I know it, but this work, it pays really well, and well, you showed me that house you wanted and—"

"Is that why you went out of town to some dangerous high-paying job? Because I wanted some house? For all I care, Sly, we can live in a hut and cook over a campfire!"

Bob and Laureen looked over, hearing Annie's raised voice, but then quickly looked away, realizing it was a personal discussion.

"Hey Annie," Sly whispered, "I just wanted to get the down payment together, then I'll be back. I'm signed on for another five months."

"Five months?"

"Yeah, but I'm done with the secrecy. We can leave the base every month, so we'll do that, okay? But then. . ."

"Then what?" Annie's voice was rising again.

"Then me and Bobby, well, we want to join the Police Force."

"Oh?"

"What do you think of that?"

"I don't know. But I think I like it. I think it suits you. So you wanna be a cop."

"Well, what we really want to do is become detectives, but you gotta do the academy before that. And then, you know, move up."

Annie smiled and snuggled into him. "My fiancé the detective," she said.

"Oh no, it'll be your husband the detective. I aint waitin' that long!"

Later, as the four girls gathered in the kitchen to put things away, Laureen came in to say a private thank you and goodbye. "I don't know what in the world we would have done without you girls."

"We're your friends," Joan said. "Of course we'd pitch in."

"You're more than friends," Laureen said, "You're my angels."

"Well if we are," Annie said, "we're angels without wings."

"Yeah," said Bernice, "Angels in the rough!"

Everyone laughed and Laureen hugged each of them, thanking them over and over.

The evening was rich with more laughter, love, and good food than anyone could ever remember. And long after the happy couple had departed, leaving only enough time to make the long drive to their Pennsylvania haven by nine o'clock, Annie, Joan, Bernice and Helen sat lingering over coffee. Bobby and Debbie and Sly talked with Harry and Dick at a separate table.

All of the happy guests had gone home, the kitchen had been cleaned, and the refrigerator emptied of all but one extra pound of butter.

"This was about the happiest day I can remember," Joan said. "For all kinds of reasons."

"Dick Thimble, being number one?" Bernice asked.

"He was the reason it could be so happy," Joan said, "but I have to say, there was something in just this getting together, all of us, having this big, important project of love for a friend to do that really fulfills me."

"I know just what you mean!" Annie said excitedly. "I was thinking of how it all came together, and we haven't been able to do this before for someone we know and love. All that time helping the soldiers and putting together the dances, it sure came in handy when we needed it for one of our own, didn't it?"

"Yeah, but I have a feeling there's another handsome reason for your happiness today, Annie," Helen said.

"I can't deny that!" Annie said, turning to look at Sly. "What a man."

"Yeah, he is. They all are," Helen said. "I better take mine home before he falls asleep." Just as she rose, Harry came over as if by some secret code.

"How do you do that?" Bernice asked.

"What?" said Helen.

"Signal him. Look, he's coming over and you haven't even called him or anything."

"He knows her," Annie said, looking at Sly.

"Either that, or he's been waiting to leave and sees his chance," Helen said chuckling.

"Well, before anybody leaves," Bernice said, "I have news."

"Uh oh!" said Annie. "Nobody's redrafted are they?"

"No. I found out why I couldn't find Margaret."

"Why is that?" Joan asked.

"Because she and Elwood eloped!"

There was a stunned silence, and then they all laughed.

"Well, so much for using these dresses for Margaret's wedding I guess!" Annie said.

"You need a lift?" Helen said to Bernice. "We brought the car."

"Sure," Bernice said. "Let me get my coat."

"You know Joanie," Annie said after they'd gone, "tonight I found out what Sly's been up to the last month."

"Oh my gosh, don't tell me it's something dangerous!"

"Yeah! But not the same way of course. He's at an installation that works on decoding secret messages, spy kind of things, and there's international bad guys trying to sabotage everything. Two guards have been shot."

"Oh Annie!"

"Yeah, but he had a good reason."

"Well, since we didn't get a chance to talk, Dick never went out with Gloria."

"I know, I knew it then."

"I know you did and I should have listened. But he says he can't marry me."

"What!"

"For three years," Joan giggled. "Law school."

"Law school? I guess that's longer than the training they'll get for the police force."

"Sly wants in at the police?"

"Yeah, them two wanna be detectives."

"Oh. Well, they'd be good ones!"

"I think so, too. I like the idea."

"So do you have to wait three years, too?"

"I don't know how long," Annie said. "I just like having him around, and now we'll see each other every month. That seems okay to me. I guess it's 'cause I know how he feels, and I know I feel the same. We're okay."

"I can't believe how much this whole thing has changed me," Joan said. "I was so desperate to be a married woman a year ago, and now I know the most important thing is that I'll marry a man I really love and who loves me. I can wait until it's the right time. In fact, there's no part of me that wants to rush anything."

"Probably after you saw all the work it was!" Annie said laughing.

Joan laughed. "It sure was! But I'm glad we did it. I feel so right doing things like that."

"I feel like we're kind of a team that people can rely on, you know, the way we rely on the men, the soldiers, the Church, everybody that serves."

"We've been lucky, but we've been protected, too. Our guardian angels have been hard at work for us this year!"

"Yes," said Annie smiling, remembering the golden winged crystal angels in her shop, and studying the men as they talked and laughed. "All the angels, including our handsome, protective, loving, tough angels in the rough."

The End.

Thank you for reading my story.
With warmest wishes,
Cece Whittaker

Angels in the Rough
Book 4 in the Serve Series by Cece Whittaker.

Find the rest of the Serve Series at:
www.CeceWhittakerStories.com

Made in the USA
Coppell, TX
05 February 2020